ST. MARTIN'S

MINOTAUR

MYSTERIES

GET A CLUE!

Be the first to hear the latest mystery book news...

With the St. Martin's Minotaur monthly newsletter,
you'll learn about the hottest new Minotaur books,
receive advance excerpts from newly published works,
read exclusive original material from featured mystery
writers, and be able to enter to win free books!

Sign up on the Minotaur Web site at:
www.minotaurbooks.com

Praise for **MARION CHESNEY** *and her* **EDWARDIAN MURDER MYSTERIES**

SICK OF SHADOWS

"A tidy and well-executed mystery/historical with strong overtones of romance."

—*Library Journal*

"A lighthearted romantic romp through Edwardian snobbery, with hints of the cataclysmic changes in store for high society."

—*Kirkus Reviews*

HASTY DEATH

"Once again Chesney has concocted an amusing brew of mystery and romance that will keep her fans turning the pages."

—*Publishers Weekly*

"If you missed the first novel in this series, get it right away. *Snobbery with Violence* introduced the Edwardian heroine Lady Rose Summer. Her second appearance is, if anything, even wittier and more amusing than the debut."

—*The Globe and Mail*

"If you are a fan of well-written traditional mysteries, Lord Peter, and Albert Campion, you might want to try this series."

—*Reviewing the Evidence*

SNOBBERY WITH VIOLENCE

"Fans of the author's Agatha Raisin and Hamish Macbeth series should welcome this tale of aristocrats, house parties, servants, and murder."

—*Publishers Weekly*

"Old hand Chesney . . . maintains her charm and sassiness while indicting evergreen pomposity and class-status stupidity."

—*Kirkus Reviews*

"Fans of the author's Hamish Macbeth and Agatha Raisin mysteries, written under the name M. C. Beaton, will welcome this new series of historical whodunits."

—*Booklist*

MORE...

"Combines history, romance, and intrigue resulting in a delightful romantic mystery."

—*Midwest Book Review*

"Light, amusing, easy to read, and thoroughly delightful."

—*The Tampa Tribune*

. . . *and for* M. C. BEATON'S AGATHA RAISIN SERIES

"Tourists are advised to watch their backs in the bucolic villages where M. C. Beaton sets her sly British mysteries. . . . Outsiders always spell trouble for the inbred societies Beaton observes with such cynical humor."

—*The New York Times Book Review*

"[Beaton's] imperfect heroine is an absolute gem!"

—*Publishers Weekly*

"Beaton's Agatha Raisin series just about defines the British cozy."

—*Booklist*

"Anyone interested in . . . intelligent, amusing reading will want to make the acquaintance of Mrs. Agatha Raisin."

—*Atlanta Journal-Constitution*

"Beaton has a winner in the irrepressible, romance-hungry Agatha."

—*Chicago Sun-Times*

"Few things in life are more satisfying than to discover a brand-new Agatha Raisin mystery."

—*Tampa Tribune Times*

"The Raisin series brings the cozy tradition back to life. God bless the Queen!"

—*Tulsa World*

"The Miss Marple–like Raisin is a refreshingly sensible, wonderfully eccentric, thoroughly likable heroine . . . a must for cozy fans."

—*Booklist*

Our Lady of Pain

MARION CHESNEY

St. Martin's Paperbacks

This is a work of fiction. All of the characters, organizations and events portrayed in this novel are either products of the author's imagination or are used fictitiously.

OUR LADY OF PAIN

Copyright © 2006 by Marion Chesney.
Excerpt from *Love, Lies and Liquor* copyright © 2007 by Marion Chesney.

Library of Congress Catalog Card Number: 2005051699

ISBN: 0-312-99837-6
EAN: 9780312-99837-0

Printed in the United States of America

St. Martin's Press hardcover edition / April 2006
St. Martin's Paperbacks edition / June 2007

St. Martin's Paperbacks are published by St. Martin's Press, 175 Fifth Avenue, New York, NY 10010.

10 9 8 7 6 5 4 3 2 1

For Sophie and Tom Lacey
and
their daughter, Tilly,
with affection

ONE

O splendid and sterile Dolores,
Our Lady of Pain

—ALGERNON CHARLES SWINBURNE

Up until that dreadful day in February, Lady Rose Summer would have sworn on a stack of Bibles that she was not a jealous woman.

She and her companion, Daisy Levine, had been suitably attired by the lady's maid to go to work: severe tweed skirts and jackets, long woollen coats, and—to the distress of Daisy—depressingly plain hats.

The fact that the Earl and Countess of Hadshire had allowed their daughter to go out to work was the result of many stormy scenes. Rose was engaged to a private detective, Captain Harry Cathcart. His previous secretary, too fond of gin, had sobered up and taken herself off to do mission work in Borneo. Rose, who had trained herself in shorthand and typing, had promptly offered to replace her.

Her parents did not know that she had an arranged engagement with Harry. Having failed a Season, they had threatened to send her off to India, the favourite destination for all failed debutantes. Horrified, Rose had begged Harry to ask for her hand in marriage.

The reason that her parents had finally capitulated was because their daughter had previously got herself into so many dangerous situations, and Harry had pointed out she would be safer under his constant protection. Daisy had promptly volunteered to act as undersecretary to guard her mistress.

The day was cold, blustery and dark as they entered Harry's office in Buckingham Palace Road.

Daisy lit the gas lamps, raked out the fire, piled up paper, kindling and coal, and soon had a cheerful blaze going.

From the shadow behind the frosted glass of the inner door, they could see Harry had already arrived. They hung up their coats, unpinned their hats and sat down at their respective desks.

Harry put his head around the door. "I have some letters for you to type. Bring your notebook, Miss Summer." It had been agreed to drop Rose's title while she was at work. "Miss Levine, you will find on your desk various bills to be sent out."

Rose sat primly in front of Harry, her notebook ready. Harry shot her an irritated glance. Despite the severity of her hairstyle, Rose was disturbingly beautiful, with her large blue eyes and clear skin. He often chafed at this odd engagement and wished to end it, but somehow could not bear to think of Rose with any other man.

He was a tall man with thick, dark hair going slightly grey at the temples. He had black eyes under heavy lids and a hard, handsome face.

Rose gave a little cough, wondering why he did not start dictating. Harry gave himself a mental shake and began the day's business as Rose's pencil flew over the shorthand pad.

When he was nearly finished, Rose heard the outer door of the office open. Then Daisy entered and said, "There's a lady to see you. A Miss Dolores Duval." She handed Harry a little visiting card.

"That will be all for now, Miss Summer," said Harry. "Show her in, Miss Levine."

A subtle scent preceded Dolores. Rose blinked at the vision that entered the room. Dolores had a curvaceous figure clad in a sky blue velvet gown. Her sable coat was thrown open. The gown was low-cut to reveal the top halves of two magnificent white breasts. On her golden hair was perched a saucy little tricorne of a hat with an ostrich plume wrapped around the top in a half circle.

Rose left them and went back to her desk. "I didn't think he did any jobs for the demi-monde," hissed Daisy. "That one's no better than she should be."

"Maybe she's an actress," suggested Rose.

"And maybe I'm the bleedin' horse's arse."

"Daisy! Language!" Daisy often slipped and revealed her Cockney origins.

A tinkling seductive laugh came from the inner office. "She's French," muttered Daisy.

Then Rose heard Harry laugh.

"I've never heard him laugh like that," exclaimed Rose.

Rose tried to type, but her fingers, usually so nimble, kept hitting the wrong keys.

Dolores seemed to be with Harry for quite a long time. At last they both emerged, Harry looking younger and happier than Rose had ever seen him appear before.

"Finish your work," ordered Harry, "and then take the rest of the day off."

He and Dolores went out and Rose and Daisy could hear them descending the stairs. Dolores's voice floated back to them. "Such a greem-looking pair of secretaries. *Tiens!* Don't they frighten you?"

They could not hear Harry's reply. They went to the window. Harry helped Dolores into her carriage and climbed in after her.

"Now, don't that worry you?" asked Daisy.

"Doesn't," corrected Rose. "Why should it? You know my engagement to the captain is merely an arrangement."

"It's an arrangement you'll soon be free of," said Daisy, "unless you're careful."

Home early?" commented the Lady Polly as her daughter walked into the drawing room. "I hope this means you've given all this silly nonsense up."

"Not at all. The captain merely had business to attend to."

"Oh, he has, has he? Well, your precious fiancé has just phoned to say he cannot escort you to the Brandons tonight because he has work to do. Such a disgrace. I have asked Jimmy Emery to escort you."

Rose felt miserable. Jimmy Emery was one of those young-men-about-town who were called on as escorts or dinner guests by people who had been let down at the last moment.

"We are not mentioned in *Queen*," said the countess, brandishing that magazine. "There is a full report of the state ball given by the king, but we are nowhere to be found in the report. It says here, 'The Countess of Dundonald wore a handsome jet-embroidered satin.' Pooh! She looked like a crow. 'The Countess of Powis looked singularly beautiful in a pale blue satin embroidered with diamonds.' No one in their right mind could call her beautiful." Jealously, Lady Polly read on. " 'Lady Ashburton was in pale blue chiffon and cloth of silver, embroidered with stripes of brilliants, the swathed bodice fastened with diamonds.' Really, I had *all* my diamonds on and my gown was one of Mr. Worth's best creations. Why have they omitted my name?" She looked up, but her daughter had silently left the room.

As a young unmarried girl who had not yet reached her majority, Rose's gowns were always white or pastel. She descended the stairs that evening to join Jimmy Emery, a tall, thin young man with his bear oil–greased hair in a centre parting.

Rose was wearing a white chiffon gown decorated at the front with two long panels of French lace. She wore white silk stockings and white kid shoes. The only colour was provided by her little gold tiara of topaz and sapphires.

As they made their way out to the earl's carriage, a thin fog was shrouding the street lamps. The earl, small and fussy and wrapped in an enormous sealskin coat, hoped loudly that it wouldn't get worse.

From under the shadow of his top hat, the earl surveyed his daughter as she sat in the carriage opposite him, flanked by her mother and Daisy. Her face was smooth and expressionless. That's what puts the fellows off, he thought. Cold as ice. No wonder she's got herself the nickname of the Ice Queen.

◆ ◆ ◆

Another hot and crowded ballroom resounding with the latest slang that the uppers cultivated to exclude the lowers. A man-man was a royal personage. Expensive was expie. A teagown was a teagie, so of course it followed that a nightgown became a nightie. Deevie meant delightful, and if you admired the cut of a friend's gown, you cried, "Fittums!" Diskie meant disgusting, and if you were one of the many fashionable ladies who borrowed money and had no intention of paying it back, you talked about lootin.' In fact, *G*'s were dropped all around and words such as saw were pronounced sawr. Although the Season was still a good way off, these early returns to London were anxious to be first in the marriage market.

Rose felt uncomfortable that voices were whispering behind fans as they looked at her saying, "She's here without her fiancé again!"

Her dance card was only half full. Although she had a large dowry, the adventurers had given up trying; the eligible young men of good family were not interested because she was engaged, and a good number of the dances had been booked by friends of her parents.

Jimmy was a good dancer, but her parents' friends were often clumsy and boring. Resentment against the absent Harry began to build up in her and reached boiling point, when, sitting out one dance with Daisy, her companion said, "I've found out all about Miss Duval. She's a famous Parisian courtesan. It's said that one man was killed in a duel over her and she left for England because she was so upset. All the men are crazy about her."

"And who is her current protector?"

"Nobody knows," said Daisy. "Becket might know." Becket was Harry's gentleman's gentleman and Daisy hoped to marry him. "Has the captain said any more about letting Becket and me marry?"

"No. You should ask him."

"I did. But he keeps saying, 'In a little while.' I thought I might see a bit of Becket now that we're working for the captain, but Becket drives him to work and then just drives off."

Both fell silent. Rose was planning to confront Harry about Dolores the next day and Daisy was going to tackle him about her marriage prospects.

The arrangement they had with Harry was that if they had been at a ball or party the night before, then they need not report for duty until midday. But both were anxious to get their problems solved and were at their desks, tired and sleepy, at nine in the morning.

No Harry.

The minutes dragged by and then the hours. They went out for a quick meal and returned at one o'clock to find Harry's office still empty.

Daisy phoned Becket but there was no reply. She put her head down on her desk and fell asleep.

Harry had suffered a leg injury during the Boer War. It was three in the afternoon before Rose heard his limping step on the stairs. She nudged Daisy awake and got to her feet as he entered.

"Any clients?" asked Harry.

"Not so far," said Rose. "I want a word with you."

He ushered her into his office. Rose confronted him. "What is your business with Miss Duval?"

"It is of a confidential nature."

"You said as part of the deal that I could help you with some of the detective work."

"Not in this case. I have been sworn to secrecy."

"It caused a fair amount of comment last night that I was once more unescorted by you."

"I'll do my best next time. Please go home. You look tired."

"Can you assure me that your dealings with Miss Duval are not of a personal nature?"

"They are strictly business, and if they were not, what is it to you? May I remind you that this so-called engagement was all your idea? Do you want to end it?"

Rose bit her lip. If she ended it with no other suitor in sight, then her parents would fulfil their threat and send her off to India.

"Not for now," she said stiffly.

"Then go home."

"Daisy wishes to speak to you."

"Very well. Send her in."

As Daisy entered the office, Harry looked at her uneasily. He knew she was going to broach the question of her possible marriage to Becket, but Becket had confided in him that he did not feel ready for marriage. Harry had rescued a man called Phil Marshall from poverty and had employed him as well as Becket. He sometimes wondered if Becket was jealous of Phil and did not want to leave and let Phil take over.

He eyed Daisy as she came in. Daisy was expensively dressed, but her green eyes held that Cockney street awareness still. She had once been a chorus girl, and despite her usually cultivated vowels he always felt that inside was a bold, raffish Daisy suppressed by gentility and the cramping confines of an Empire corset.

"What are you doing about me marrying Becket?" asked Daisy.

Harry suppressed a sigh. He decided that Becket would just have to handle this himself. "I think you should speak to Becket yourself," he said.

Daisy's eyes widened in alarm. "What's up?"

"I really think Becket should tell you himself." Harry rang his home in Chelsea and ordered Becket to come to the office immediately. He put down the phone and said, "He'll be here soon. You may use my office. I am going out now."

Rose, when she heard the news, said she would wait for Daisy.

She watched sadly as Harry nodded to her before going out. She remembered the way he had kissed her and how everything had seemed wonderful. But ever since that kiss, he had retreated into his usual cold shell.

Becket arrived and Daisy took him into Harry's office. "Why's nothing been said about us getting married?" demanded Daisy.

Becket was a neat precise man with pale regular features and neatly cut and greased hair.

"I don't think the captain's ready to release me," he said.

Daisy studied him for a long moment. "So why didn't the captain tell me? It's not like him to leave you to speak to me." Servants, however high up, were used to their employers behaving like parents.

Becket studied the floor. There was a long silence.

The gaslight hissed and popped in its bracket. A coal shifted in the fireplace. The yellow-faced clock on the wall ticked busily.

"Fact is," said Becket at last, "I don't feel quite ready for marriage."

Daisy's face flamed. "Then you can make a noise like a hoop and bowl off. Be damned to you, you stupid lying bastard!"

She flew out of the office. "Come on," she said to Rose. "Let's get out of here."

Rose put on her coat and hat. "We'll go across the road for some tea and you can tell me all about it."

Becket walked out past them, his head down.

They locked the door and went out. When they were settled in the café across the road, Daisy blurted out that Becket no longer wanted to marry her and then burst into noisy tears. Rose patted her back and made comforting noises. At last, Daisy blew her nose and then scrubbed her eyes dry with a clean handkerchief handed to her by Rose.

Then she realized Rose was staring across the road.

A carriage had arrived. Rose recognized that carriage. "Wait here!" she ordered Daisy. She went out and crossed the street. She considered hiding in a doorway until she realized that the couple descending from the carriage were unaware of her existence.

Harry helped Dolores to alight. She smiled up at him from under the brim of a hat trimmed with pink silk roses. Harry smiled back. Then he offered her his arm and led her towards his office.

Jealousy raged in Rose's bosom but she did not recognize the emotion as jealousy. She considered it righteous anger. By being seen so publicly with such a well-known courtesan, Harry was not only damaging his reputation, but, by association, hers as well.

For once Daisy, wrapped in her own misery, was deaf to her mistress's complaints.

There was not very much social life in London before the Season. But there were calls to make and little supper parties to go to. And at each event, Rose received sly digs from the other ladies about her fiancé having been seen so often with Dolores.

The crunch came for Rose when she attended the opera with her parents and Daisy. Her parents only attended the opera because it was the thing to do and both were apt to fall asleep when the first note of the overture sounded.

Looking across at the other boxes, Rose suddenly stiffened with shock. Harry had just entered a box opposite with Dolores. She was wearing a golden silk gown with a heavy diamond-and-ruby necklace. A diamond tiara flashed on her blonde hair. Rose wondered bitterly which ladies of Paris had found their jewels missing after their doting husbands had given them to Dolores.

Her heart sank even further when her father suddenly exclaimed, "There's Cathcart in the box opposite with that French tart!"

The countess fumbled for her opera glasses, raised them to her eyes and hissed, "Disgraceful. Rose, he will be summoned and you will break off your ridiculous engagement. Peggy Struthers is going to India with her gel. I'll ask her to chaperone you."

"I do not want to go to India!"

"You will do as you're told."

Rose could not pay attention to the opera. Dolores

was flirting boldly and Harry seemed to be enjoying every moment of it.

At the interval, when everyone mingled in the crush bar, Lord Hadshire approached Harry, drew him aside and muttered, "Your presence is requested tomorrow at eleven o'clock. No, don't say a word."

Dolores had left Harry's side to speak to some men. Rose followed her and as she turned away to rejoin Harry, Rose said loudly and clearly, "Leave my fiancé alone, you bitch, or I'll kill you!"

There was a sudden shocked silence.

"That's it!" said Lady Polly furiously, joining her daughter. "We're going home."

Rose barely slept that night. She tossed and turned, wondering all the while how she could stop her parents' sending her to India. Parents of failed debutantes always hoped that their hitherto unmarriageable daughters would become marriageable when out in India and surrounded by lonely men far from home.

At last, Rose decided boldness was the only answer. The only record of Dolores she had been able to find in the office was her address in Cromwell Gardens in Kensington.

She would go there in the morning and confront Dolores and find out what was going on.

Daisy was alarmed when she heard Rose's plan the next morning. "Don't come with me," said Rose. "Go to the office, and if the captain asks, say I am unwell."

Not wanting to occasion comment by taking one of her father's carriages, Rose hailed a hack and directed the driver to Kensington.

She paid off the hack in Cromwell Gardens and stood looking up at the house. Could Dolores really afford a whole house? But on approaching the door, she found it had been divided up into four flats, and Dolores's name was on a card indicating that she lived in a house made up of two flats, one on the ground floor and one above.

Rose pulled the white bell stop. She waited and waited. Then she tried the handle of the front door. It was unlocked. She went into a large square hall. A cleaning woman was on her hands and knees scrubbing the floor.

"Which is Miss Duval's flat?" asked Rose.

"Door on your left, missus," said the woman over her shoulder.

The door was slightly open. Rose knocked and then called. No reply. She stepped inside the flat. She would leave her card on a tray she could see on the side table. She took out her card case, and then put it away again. Dolores might only be amused by the fact she had called. Then she saw the door to a front parlour was open. She walked towards it. Perhaps there might be some evidence of why Dolores had hired Harry.

The first thing she saw was one slippered foot lying behind a sofa by the window. Her heart began to thud. Rose walked around the sofa and let out a sharp scream of fright. Dolores was lying dead on the floor. She was dressed only in a white silk-and-lace nightgown and an elaborately embroidered dressing gown. A red stain of blood had seeped from a hole in her chest. A revolver was lying on the floor beside her. Numb with shock, Rose picked up the revolver.

A loud scream erupted from behind her. Rose

swung round, eyes dilated with fright, the revolver still
in her hand. It was the cleaning woman. "Murder!" she
screeched and then ran out into the street, shouting,
"Murder. Perlees! Murder!"

People began to crowd in to Dolores's flat. Rose
stared at them and they stared at Rose until a man
walked forward and took the revolver from her.

"What's going on here?" A policeman thrust his
way through the crowd. A chorus of voices rose, some
shouting, "She murdered her. She had the gun in her
hand."

"I didn't . . . I found her," whispered Rose through
white lips.

"Name?"

"Lady Rose Summer."

The policeman turned and shooed everyone out of
the flat. He saw a telephone on a table by the fireplace
and dialled Scotland Yard.

M y business with Miss Duval is confidential,"
Harry was saying to the enraged earl.

"You paraded yourself and that trollop at the opera
in front of everyone. Your engagement to my daughter
is off. What is it, Jarvis?"

The earl's secretary was hovering nervously in the
doorway.

"I beg your pardon, my lord, but I have received an
urgent call from Scotland Yard. Lady Rose has been
arrested for murder."

TWO

A little sincerity is a dangerous thing,
and a great deal of it is absolutely fatal.

—OSCAR WILDE

Superintendent Kerridge knew Rose. She had been involved in several of his previous cases. He had her escorted to his office and served with hot sweet tea, anxious to interrogate her quickly, as he was sure the earl was about to descend on him with a battalion of lawyers.

Kerridge was a grey man: grey hair, grey bushy eyebrows, grey face, and all set off with a grey suit. He had a soft spot for Lady Rose, probably because he sensed a misfit like himself. Inside Kerridge burned a dreamer who would like to see the aristocracy hanging from the lamp posts. But he kept his views to himself. He had a wife and children to look after.

"Now, my lady," he began, "tell me exactly what happened and why you were there."

"I saw Harry—Captain Cathcart—at the opera with Miss Duval. He had told me he was investigating something for her, but I felt he was disgracing me by association. He had no right to appear to be escorting her. I went to have it out with her. The door was open. When I walked in, I saw a foot protruding from behind the sofa. I walked round. She was dead. Shot. I screamed. There was a revolver lying next to her. I was dazed with shock. I picked it up and then the cleaning woman rushed in and began crying murder."

There came the sounds of a loud altercation outside and Kerridge damned the advent of the motor car, which got people from point A to point B so quickly.

A police officer put his head around the door. "Sir, Lord Hadshire is here—" he had begun when he was rudely thrust aside. The earl bustled in, followed by his wife, Lady Polly, Captain Harry, and Sir Crispin Briggs, Q.C.

"Don't say another word," the earl barked at his daughter.

"Has she been charged?" asked Briggs.

"Not yet," said Kerridge heavily. "I had just begun to interrogate her."

"Then if you wish to ask her any more questions, you can do it at our house with Sir Harry Briggs present."

Kerridge sighed. "Then I shall visit you this afternoon. I have witnesses to interview. Captain Cathcart. A word with you."

He waited until Rose was bundled out by her parents and barrister.

Harry sat down and looked at Kerridge bleakly. "What on earth was Rose up to?"

"It seems the final straw came when you squired Miss Duval to the opera. Lady Rose went to confront Miss Duval. She says she found her dead, and in a moment of shock, picked up the revolver. She was found like that by the cleaning woman and several other witnesses. It looks bad."

"Fingerprints?"

"Sent over to the Bureau already. So what was Miss Duval's business with you?"

"Miss Duval had received various threatening letters. She wanted me to find out who had written them and to protect her until such time as I found out the culprit."

"Why did she not go to the police?"

"She begged me not to. She had a fear of the police. Miss Duval had been in some trouble in Paris. A certain aristocratic lady claimed that Miss Duval had stolen a pearl necklace. Miss Duval said that the necklace had been given to her by the lady's husband. It was a great scandal and she said she received rough treatment from the police and the newspapers."

"Do you have the letters?"

"Miss Duval kept them at her flat."

"What were the threats like?"

"Things like, 'I am coming to kill you. Your sort of woman shouldn't be alive.' Written on cheap paper."

Kerridge stood up. "We'd better get to Kensington as soon as possible. I must see these letters."

"Becket will drive us. He's waiting downstairs."

Becket was silent and miserable during the drive. Rose in trouble meant Daisy would be drawn into possible danger. He wished he had told Daisy the whole truth of his fear of marriage. Marriage would mean leaving the captain's employ, where he had been so secure, and venturing into the world of business because the captain had promised to set him up in some trade. Becket had been poor when the captain had rescued him and he dreaded failing in business and returning to a life of poverty. Then Phil Marshall, also rescued by the captain and working for him, had been excited at the idea of taking over Becket's job, and was plainly upset and disappointed when Becket showed no signs of leaving. Daisy had initially suggested that they set up a dress salon using costumes designed by Lady Polly's seamstress, Miss Friendly. But Becket felt it was somehow not a *manly* job. He preferred setting up a pub, but Daisy had balked at the idea of pulling pints.

"Look out!" shouted Harry. "Pay attention, Becket. You nearly ran over that man."

At Cromwell Gardens, Kerridge nodded to the policemen, who were still taking statements from the cleaning woman and the neighbours, and went into the flat. The pathologist, who had been kneeling beside the body, rose up at their arrival.

"Clean shot right through the heart," he said. "No signs of a struggle."

Detective Inspector Judd entered. "Doesn't seem to be any break-in or tampering with the locks. It was someone she knew."

"We're looking for threatening letters that the captain here said were sent to her. Let's start."

They all searched diligently, but there was no sign of the letters. They were just about to give up when a sharp voice cried out, "What is going on? What are you doing here?"

They all swung round. A tall, severe-looking woman stood in the doorway to the front parlour.

Harry recognized her. "The lady's maid," he said quickly to Kerridge. "Miss Thomson, I am afraid I have bad news for you. Your mistress has been murdered."

Miss Thomson sank down onto the nearest chair, her hand at her throat. "Those letters," she said. "I told her to go to the police." Her voice had a Scottish burr.

"Why were you absent from the house?" asked Kerridge. "And what about the other servants?"

"Miss Duval insisted we all take the day off."

"Who works here apart from yourself?"

"There's the parlourmaid, Ralston; the cook-housekeeper, Mrs. Jackson; the kitchen maid, Betty; and Mrs. Anderson, who comes in three times a week to do the rough. Mrs. Anderson is here. She says she came back for something. The rest will all be back by early evening. How was my mistress murdered?"

"Miss Duval was shot. Did she say anything about expecting a visitor?"

"Miss Duval did not. But I had the feeling she was going to entertain someone she did not want us to see."

"Have you any idea who that person might be?"

"I thought it might be a certain royal personage."

"Keep that thought to yourself," snapped Kerridge. Dear God! Was he going to have to interview the king?

"How long have you been in the employ of Miss Duval?"

"Ever since madam came to London. She got rid of her French staff. She did not trust them and suspected one of them of sending snippets about her to the newspapers."

"So when did she come to London?"

"Only a month ago," said Harry.

"And how did she hire the staff?"

"Madam hired the others through an agency. She had advertised for a lady's maid in the *Times* before leaving Paris. I applied for the post."

"Your previous employer?"

"Lady Burridge."

"And why did you leave?"

"Lady Burridge died."

"Now, we are looking for threatening letters sent to Miss Duval. Do you know where she kept them?"

"Certainly. She kept them in a little bureau in the boudoir upstairs."

"Show us."

Harry and Kerridge followed the lady's maid's erect figure up the stairs. "Why did you choose to work for a member of the demi-monde?" asked Kerridge.

She turned on the landing. "Miss Duval paid good wages and was kind. I shall miss her."

She led the way into a pretty boudoir and went straight to the bureau. "Oh, that one," said Kerridge gloomily. "That's already been searched."

"There are no signs of a frantic search," said Harry. "There were no drawers pulled out and left open. Neither was the outer door forced. It looks as if Miss Duval knew her visitor, may even have confided in this visitor and shown him the letters. What about her jewels? And why was she clad only in her nightgown and dressing gown? It looks as if she was expecting a lover."

"Madam fretted at the restriction of stays. She went around clad only in her undress most mornings. I tried to persuade her to wear something more seemly, but she laughed at me and called me a fuddy-duddy." Thomson sat down as if her legs had suddenly given way. She pulled out a handkerchief and dabbed at her eyes.

"Jewels!" said Harry sharply. "Has anything been taken?"

Thomson went to a large jewel box. "The key is in the lock," she said. "That's odd. It is always kept locked. I have one key and madam had the other."

She threw open the lid. Inside were a series of trays with rings and earrings. She lifted them out. In the well of the box were piles of necklaces. "Madam kept her diamonds at the bank," said Thomson. "But there is a sapphire necklace, a ruby necklace and a necklace of black pearls missing."

"You are sure?" asked Kerridge.

"I check the inventory every evening. Also I made a daily inventory of the lace box." Lace was in vogue for trimmings and some of it was priceless.

"Why is there dust over everything?" asked Thomson.

"Men from the fingerprint bureau dusted everything for prints before we began our search."

Kerridge hated to ask the next question, but he knew where his duty lay. "Why did you assume this visitor might be a royal personage?"

"It was something madam said. We had been shopping at Fortnum's. There was a particular tea they sell that madam liked. His Majesty visited the store while we were there. He seemed much taken with my mistress. He drew her aside and whispered something to her. Madam blushed and laughed and for the rest of that day was very elated."

"But she didn't say anything specific?"

Thomson shook her head.

"Friends? Did she have a particular friend she may have confided in?"

"Not that I know of."

"Gentlemen friends?"

"Only Captain Cathcart."

"Very well, Miss Thomson. You may retire. We will wait for the rest of the staff to arrive."

When she had gone, Kerridge eyed Harry suspiciously. "Were your relations with Miss Duval strictly business?"

"Yes. I was protecting her and trying to find out who had sent the letters."

"I tell you what's odd," said Kerridge heavily. "Here's a famous French tart whose business it is to find herself a wealthy protector. But the only person around is you."

"Miss Duval told me she did not wish to . . . er . . . return to business until whoever had written those letters had been found."

"What was she like?"

"I would estimate she was at the top of her profession. You see, it's not just what they do in bed, it is how they can charm and entertain out of it. She was warmhearted, witty and funny. I liked her immensely."

"Liked? That was all?"

"Yes."

Kerridge took out a large pocket watch. "We had better go and interview Lady Rose."

Harry felt low during the drive to the earl's. He had not been quite honest with Kerridge. He had been charmed and fascinated by Dolores. Apart from her charm and her undoubted sexual attraction, she had exuded an almost maternal warmth. He felt guilty when he thought about Rose. Yes, he had kissed Rose passionately and she had responded, but when he had seen her again, she had seemed cold and remote. It had not dawned on Harry that the normally courageous Rose was shy. The newspapers tomorrow were going to crucify her. He was sure the neighbours who had found her with the revolver had already talked, not to mention the cleaning woman.

No one had thought to tell Daisy of the day's events. She had interviewed a gentleman who wanted proof of his wife's adultery and two ladies who were distressed over their missing pets.

Feeling very much in charge, Daisy decided to tackle the cases herself, setting out in pursuit of the missing pets and resolving to start a watch on the gentleman's wife the next day.

Accompanied by the barrister, Briggs, Rose was taken through her story again. She was white and shaken. Harry longed to comfort her, but she did not look at him once. Instead, he said to the earl, "Someone was sending Miss Duval threatening letters. They have disappeared. I am sure that person is the one who murdered her."

Lady Polly said, "Oh, Rose, if only you hadn't threatened to kill the woman yourself."

"What's this?" asked Kerridge sharply.

"You need not answer any more questions," said Briggs quickly.

"I may as well tell him," said Rose sadly. "There were so many witnesses. My fiancé escorted Miss Duval to the opera. I was incensed. I felt he was tarnishing our relationship by consorting publicly with a doxy. I went up to her in the crush bar at the interval and I said something like, 'Leave my fiancé alone, you bitch, or I'll kill you.'"

"Oh, why on earth did you say such a thing?" mourned Harry.

She looked at him for the first time. "I should not have said it. Neither you nor she were worth the effort."

"I think we're finished here," said Briggs.

"Yes, go to your room," said Lady Polly.

Harry watched her go. He would never have dreamed that anything he did could rouse Rose to a jealous fury. Perhaps she loved him after all. But she would never forgive him for having taken Dolores to the opera. He should never have let Dolores talk him into it.

Looks right bad for Lady Rose," said Kerridge as Becket drove them to Scotland Yard. "The earl was a fool to stop us searching her rooms. If she hasn't got that jewellery, then it's a good step towards getting her in the clear."

"You can get a search warrant."

"For an earl's town house? I'll be blocked at every turn."

"I'll need to persuade them to send Lady Rose away somewhere. Once the newspapers come out tomorrow, she will be damned as a murderess and there'll be a mob at her door."

"She will certainly be featured largely in the papers but not damned. I don't think so in this case."

"Why?"

"If Lady Rose had killed a respectable lady, it would

be another matter. But her fiancé has been seen squiring around a French tart. It will be regarded as a crime of passion. You may find yourself, and not Lady Rose, the villain on the piece."

Daisy returned home. She sensed something was up as soon as Brum, the butler, answered the door to her. Daisy had the front door key but was not expected to use it except in an emergency. She had been reprimanded for using the key on one occasion by Lady Polly, who had said, "Why open doors when servants are paid to do so?"

"Hullo, Brum," said Daisy. "Why the long face?"

He shook his head and said portentously, "Bad times."

Daisy threw him an alarmed look and darted up the stairs to Rose's private sitting room.

Rose was sitting in an armchair in front of a smouldering fire, a book lying open on her lap. Daisy saw immediately that Rose had been crying. She knelt down beside her. "What's the matter? Tell Daisy."

In a tired flat voice, Rose told her about the murder and about her involvement in finding the body.

She finished by saying, "I am really ruined now. It will be in all the newspapers tomorrow. My engagement to the captain is over. If I don't find someone quickly to marry me, we will be sent off to India. That is, if I don't end up in prison."

"We could run away," said Daisy. "You've got loads of jewels. We could sell them and go to Scotland or Ireland or somewhere like that. I know, we could go back to the Shufflebottoms in Yorkshire." Rose and Daisy had been sent to stay with Bert Shufflebottom, a village policeman, the year before, when Rose's life had been in danger.

Rose shook her head. "Mr. Shufflebottom is a policeman. If it was found out he was harbouring us, he would lose his job."

"We could ask Miss Friendly for suggestions. She told me that before her father ran through all the money, they used to travel."

"We cannot involve her." Rose had rescued Miss Friendly from a life of genteel poverty and had employed her as a seamstress almost around the same time as Harry had rescued Phil Marshall from destitution. She remembered thinking their similar actions had formed a bond between them, and felt like crying again.

"I cannot face tomorrow," said Rose, "but where can we go?"

"Perhaps some seaside town. We could stay in a quiet hotel. It's out of season. There won't be many folks around."

"I do have a certain amount of money at the bank," said Rose slowly. "I could draw it out tomorrow. It would occasion too much comment if I tried to sell my jewels. The jeweller might feel obliged to contact my father. A reputable jeweller would be sure to ask how I had come by them and a disreputable one would not give us value. If you remember, my Aunt Matilda died a few months ago and left me a tidy sum. But how will we get out of the house tomorrow with all the press on the doorstep and the servants watching my every move?"

Daisy frowned in thought. Then she said, "They'll

assume I have gone to work. I'll get into your bed and pretend to be you and say I'm not feeling well and wish to be left alone."

"But if I go to the bank with stories about me all over the newspapers and draw out money, the manager may well phone my father."

Daisy sat back on her heels. "I've got it," she said. "There's quite a bit of money in the safe in the office."

"Pa's money! No, we couldn't."

"Yes, we could. I'll rob it and leave a note saying we'll pay back everything when the fuss has died down. That way, it wouldn't *really* be stealing."

"But luggage! How do we get it out of the house?"

"We'll pack up tonight and when everyone's asleep, I'll leave it behind the shed in the garden and put a ladder against the garden wall."

"How will you get into the safe?"

"Easy. Matthew Jarvis has the key in a desk in his office. It isn't one of the newfangled ones with a dial."

"And where will we go?"

"We'll go to Paddington and take a train somewhere. You'll need to be heavily veiled so that no one recognizes you."

"I'm such a coward," said Rose. "But I cannot face the captain. I cannot face seeing the press outside the door."

"So we'll do it," said Daisy, hoping privately that Becket would be so alarmed at her disappearance that he might come to his senses.

As dawn was breaking, Rose and Daisy sat in a first-class carriage as the train to a small seaside resort called Thurby-on-Sea pulled out of Paddington station. Rose could only be glad that they had the compartment to themselves because the heavy veil she was wearing was stifling her. Daisy lowered the blinds on the corridor windows. "I brought a packed lunch," she said. "We daren't go into the dining room because you'd need to raise your veil to eat."

The train roared south, Rose lowering her veil every time it stopped at a station in case someone joined them in the compartment, but they were left alone until they reached Thurby-on-Sea.

"Why Thurby-on-Sea?" asked Rose wearily as they finally stood on a small windswept platform.

"I've never heard of it," said Daisy cheerfully, "so I suppose most people haven't either. Porter!"

O nce settled in a cab, they asked the driver to take them to a good hotel. He drove to the Thurby Palace, which was smaller than its grand name suggested. It was situated on a promenade along which a gale whipped with increasing ferocity.

Daisy checked them in under the names of the Misses Callendar. "Why Callendar?" whispered Rose.

"It just came to me," Daisy whispered back. "I used to dance with a Scotch girl who came from there." Daisy had once been a chorus girl.

They were ushered into two bedchambers with a sitting room in between.

Rose walked to the window of the sitting room and looked out at the plunging waves, which were now sending spray up over the promenade.

"It's cold in here," complained Daisy. She pulled the

bell rope beside the fireplace, and when the porter answered the summons asked him to light the fires.

He looked curiously at the heavily veiled figure of Rose standing by the window.

"Get on with it," snapped Daisy.

They waited until he had left. Rose unpinned her hat and veil and sat down by the sitting room fire, stretching her hands out to the blaze.

"I brought some stuff from the masquerade box," said Daisy. "I'll disguise you so that we can go down to the dining room and get something to eat. It's just noon."

Rose stifled a yawn. The train had taken four hours, stopping at innumerable tiny stations before creaking into Thurby-on-Sea on the Essex coast.

Daisy was unlocking their luggage. "Here!" she said triumphantly. She held up a grey wig and a pair of spectacles. "Put these on. No one will recognize you from your photo in the newspapers."

"Is my photo in the newspapers?"

"Bound to be, but I thought it would be best if you didn't know what they were writing about you. I've got a wig for meself," said Daisy. "The minute we're found missing, the police'll be looking for me as well."

What have I done? thought Rose, suddenly appalled. We have robbed my father and run away. I am a coward. What will Captain Cathcart think of me?

She suddenly remembered Dolores Duval's dead body and burst into overwrought tears.

"There, there, I'm here," cooed Daisy.

"I-I am s-such a weakling," sobbed Rose.

"Now, then, it's only for a few days, until those dreadful press people have given up."

Rose dried her eyes and turned a white face up to Daisy. "But I have just realized that in running away, I will now make Mr. Kerridge sure that I am guilty."

Daisy looked at her uneasily. Then she said bracingly, "Food is what we need. We didn't have any breakfast. Let's put on our disguises and go downstairs. Have you ever seen such an old-fashioned set of rooms? I don't think they've been changed for half a century."

The sitting room was overfurnished. The mantel was draped with cloth and the chairs were also draped with long cloth covers to hide their embarrassing legs. The Victorians of the last century had even found the sight of naked chair legs slightly disreputable. A badly executed oil painting of Queen Victoria glared down at them accusingly.

Rose went through to one of the bedrooms and sat down at the dressing table. She arranged the grey wig over her hair and put on the glasses, which had unmagnified lenses. Daisy came in carrying two hats. "I packed us two of the most dowdy ones. Don't want to occasion comment by looking too smart."

They waited until they heard the luncheon gong sound and then went down the stairs and into the dining room. Rose heaved a sigh of relief. The only other diners were an elderly couple.

Daisy shook out her napkin. "I hope the food's not too bad," she said. "I really don't think a dump in a backwater like this can afford a good cook."

The meal came as a pleasant surprise. They started with a good vegetable broth followed by poached haddock and then tucked into a large dish of roast beef and Yorkshire pudding. The dessert was spotted dick with custard.

"Goodness," said Daisy when they had finished. "Can't wait to get upstairs and take me stays off."

The elderly lady and her husband exchanged shocked glances.

"Do be quiet, Daisy," hissed Rose. "You're drawing attention to us."

But it was a relief to be back in their rooms again and to be able to undress and climb into their respective beds.

Rose's last thought before she fell asleep was of Harry. He would be so angry with her.

THREE

So, naturalists observe, a flea
Hath smaller fleas that on him prey;
And these have smaller fleas to bite 'em,
And so proceed ad infinitum.

—JONATHAN SWIFT

"You what?"

Kerridge shifted uneasily but stared defiantly at the head of Scotland Yard, Sir Ian Wetherby.

"The lady's maid, Thomson, thought that Miss Duval might have been expecting a visit from a royal personage."

"Drop that line of investigation immediately, do you hear?"

"Yes, sir. But this is murder."

"Leave it alone. Why are you fiddling about with this? Lady Rose Summer is found standing over a body with a gun in her hand. Arrest her."

"Her lawyer is Sir Crispin Briggs. He would point out we hadn't a case. Jewellery was stolen. The fingerprints on the gun are those of Lady Rose, but also there are other fingerprints as well."

"I am surprised Hadshire let you fingerprint his precious daughter."

"We lifted her fingerprints from her office desk and typewriter."

"I still think she's done it. Probably had an accomplice. Go and interview her again. I still think we have a good case against her but I will leave it to your discretion."

Meaning, thought Kerridge, that if I make a mistake, it's all my fault.

So on the morning of Rose's flight, Kerridge fought his way through the questioning press to the earl's front door and knocked loudly. He had taken the precaution of telephoning to say he was coming. The door opened a crack and then wider as Brum recognized the visitor. A babble of questions shouted by the press followed Kerridge indoors.

"Pray inform his lordship that I wish to speak to Lady Rose again."

Brum went off up the stairs. Kerridge waited a long time. Brum finally came back down and said, "His lordship is now prepared to see you."

The earl was seated in the morning room with Lady Polly. "I think it necessary to interview Lady Rose again."

"You'll need to wait till Briggs gets here."

The door opened and Brum reappeared. "My lord, Hunter informs me that neither Lady Rose nor Miss Levine are in their rooms and they have taken luggage." Hunter was Rose's lady's maid.

He was followed by an agitated Matthew Jarvis. "The money's gone from the safe, my lord. This note was lying in it."

The earl took the note and scrutinized it. It was from

Daisy. It said bluntly, "We have run away. The money will be replaced when we return. Yr. Humble and Obedient Servant, Daisy Levine."

"Get Cathcart!" howled the earl.

"This is very bad, my lord," said Kerridge. "Sir Ian Wetherby already considers Lady Rose to be guilty. Her running away will only confirm it."

"Captain Cathcart," announced Brum in tones of doom.

"That was quick," said the earl. "I've only just told Matthew to get you."

"I was already on my way." Harry looked round at the strained faces. "What's up?"

"Lady Rose has run away," said Kerridge.

"How could she be so stupid?" raged Harry. "If the press gets to hear of this, she'll be as good as hanged in tomorrow's papers. Kerridge, we must get her back before this gets out."

Kerridge said, "Do you remember last year when we had to smuggle them out of the house? They went out over the garden wall at the back."

"Come on," said Harry, "let's look. My lord, make sure none of your servants breathes a word of this to the press."

In the garden they found the ladder propped against the wall. "We'll go to the nearest cab rank," said Kerridge. "They must have taken a hack somewhere. I'll put out an alert that all ports and stations are to be watched."

"If you do that, when she returns you will be obliged to arrest her. Let me find her and bring her back," pleaded Harry.

"I could lose my job."

"If Wetherby asks, tell him she's had a nervous breakdown and you need to wait to see her again."

Kerridge sighed. "I'll give you a couple of days. I can't hold out longer than that."

By diligent questioning, working all day and long into the evening, Harry traced them as far as Paddington station. A porter remembered two ladies, one heavily veiled and one cheeky one. He had put their luggage on the train and he'd heard the cheeky one saying they were going to Thurby-on-Sea. Harry checked the timetable. There were no trains to Thurby-on-Sea until early morning the next day. He returned to his car parked outside the station and said to Becket, "I've found out where they've gone. Thurby-on-Sea. We'll set out first thing in the morning. I'm bone-weary. I need some sleep. It'll be better if we drive instead of taking the train."

"They may have journeyed on from Thurby," said Becket anxiously.

"I know the place. It's a dead-alive hole. They won't be going any further. I need to let my anger calm down or I'll strangle Lady Rose."

"Perhaps I could go myself," suggested Becket. "I don't mind driving through the night."

"No, Becket."

Rose and Daisy went back up to their rooms after breakfast the next morning. It had been raining during the night and the wind still howled with dreadful ferocity. They locked the doors and took off their disguises.

"I'm bored," said Rose. "It's like being under some

sort of genteel house arrest. I know, I put some books
in the bottom of my trunk."

Rose had not completely unpacked. She searched
through clothes and underwear, and then sat back on
her heels with a cry of alarm.

Daisy came to join her. Lying in the bottom of the
trunk beside three books was a bundle of letters. Rose
selected one. It read, "Trollops like you shouldn't be
allowed to live. I'm coming to get you." Rose picked
up one after the other, reading feverishly.

"These are the threatening letters," she said, turning a white face to Daisy. "Someone put them in my
luggage."

"What threatening letters?"

"Captain Cathcart said something about someone
sending threatening letters to Miss Duval. He then said
the letters were now missing. What are they doing in
my luggage?"

"Someone's trying to get you accused of the murder," said Daisy.

"Whoever it is must have been watching and followed us," said Rose. "There are very few guests. Did
you notice anyone in particular?"

Daisy furrowed her brow. "Let me see. Last night
was busier. There was that elderly couple; a travelling
salesman, or said he was, talked loudly to the couple; a
spinster-looking lady and a sort of youngish man."

"What was he like? The young man?"

"I didn't notice him much. Only a quick glance. He
was seated at the table behind us. How would anyone
recognize us with our disguises?"

"Someone who was watching the house and followed us from London. We'll need to find somewhere

else," said Rose frantically. "And what do we do with these letters? If he can find us, the police can find us."

"Burn them," said Daisy, looking at the fire.

"They're evidence!"

"They're evidence against you!"

The door burst open and Rose let out a scream of terror. Harry Cathcart, tired and furious, having set out before dawn after a restless night, strode into the room. "What the blazes are you doing? Don't you know you made yourself look even guiltier by fleeing? What's that you're holding?" He snatched the letters from Rose. "Where did you get those?"

"I found them this morning," said Rose. "I was going to unpack and there they were in the bottom of my trunk."

"So someone followed you. Wait here."

Harry rushed out again.

Rose was beginning to feel irrationally angry. He should have said something like, "Thank God, you are safe." Not berated her as if she were a guilty schoolgirl.

"Listen," said Daisy. "The wind has dropped suddenly."

"I'm nervous waiting here. Don't you see, Daisy, that whoever tried to make me look guilty did the murder himself? So there is a murderer in this hotel."

"If he'd wanted to kill us, he would have done so already," said Daisy. "All he wanted to do was make you look guilty."

Harry came back. "I've checked the hotel register. One man called Mr. Terence Cramley left this morning. The others all seem respectable. I'll go out and search the town for him. I've got a description. I'll call at the station and see if he's taken a train. Kerridge gave me only two days to find you. Pack up your things. We've got to get out of here."

Kerridge was summoned that morning by Sir Ian Wetherby. "I have just sustained a visit from His Majesty's equerry, Lord Herring," began Wetherby. "His Majesty wishes all inquiries into the death of Dolores Duval to continue quietly. I believe the editors of the newspapers have all been informed. His Majesty is distressed that Lady Rose should even be considered guilty." The earl's been busy, thought Kerridge cynically. "I also received a telephone call from the prime minister," Wetherby went on. "He suggests that as Miss Duval was no better than she should be, to quote his words, then it stands to reason that some low life got rid of her."

"What about the so-called freedom of the press?" asked Kerridge.

"These editors have probably all been told that a knighthood may be in the offing if they behave themselves. A statement is to be issued tomorrow in all the newspapers to say the police have found Lady Rose to be innocent of any crime."

"It is lucky that I believe that to be true. What if it turns out that our royal personage was involved in some way?"

"Piffle. Absolute piffle. I prefer to forget you even said that, Kerridge. Now go about your business."

Harry found no trace of the mysterious Mr. Cramley in Thurby-on-Sea. He returned to the hotel and told Rose and Daisy to be ready to leave.

Rose hesitated on the steps of the hotel. A watery sunlight was shining on the choppy sea and the wind had died down. She wished in that moment that Harry had not found her so quickly. Oh, for just a few days away from the press and the gossip of society!

"Come along," barked Harry.

"Yes, sir," said Rose and gave him a mock salute. Harry glared at her. She should be ashamed, contrite, over all the trouble she had caused him.

Rose, wrapped up in a bearskin rug and with her veil tied down over her hat, sat in the passenger seat of Harry's Rolls Royce as they cruised along the streets of London. Harry was driving and Becket and Daisy were in the back.

A thin mist was swirling among the narrow sooty streets. Women, wearing the enormous hats which were so fashionable, hurried along like so many animated mushrooms. Moisture from the mist made the sooty buildings on either side glisten like jet. The air smelt of horse manure, bad drains, patchouli and baking bread.

Harry, who had maintained an angry silence during the journey, broke it to ask, "What were your parents about, to come to London during such an unfashionable period?"

"My mother gets bored in the country. They would not let me work for you unless they were in London as well. Where are you going? This is not the way home."

"We are going straight to Scotland Yard. Kerridge will want to see you. Once you are home, he will not have a chance. You will no doubt have to begin preparations to go to India."

"But I am engaged to you!"

"Your father was just terminating the engagement when the news came that you had been found standing over a dead body with a gun in your hand."

"I *can't* go!"

"It might be best for all of us. You can no longer work for me. The press will follow your every move."

Rose realized for the first time that before, she had always had a certain hold on him, and she sensed miserably that that hold had gone.

Kerridge greeted them with relief. "I had better telephone your parents to say you are safe and well."

"Before you do that," said Harry, "let's discuss this." He took out the bundle of threatening letters and explained to Kerridge how they had been found.

"So we can put a face to this man. What did he look like?"

"Unfortunately, the staff at the hotel could only give a scrappy description. Possibly in his mid-thirties, slight Cockney accent, white face, pinched features, thin brown hair, and wearing a dark blue coat and trousers. I searched Thurby and checked the station. There was no sign of him. He had checked into the hotel for only one night."

"Why didn't you telephone so that I could have alerted the local police?"

"There had been gales and the telephone lines had come down."

"Wait here. I'll get on to it right away."

Rose sat wrapped in miserable thoughts. She re-

membered talking to a certain Mrs. Dursley at an afternoon tea party. Mrs. Dursely had been an unsuccessful
debutante who had been packed off to India. She had
married Colonel Dursley, a man old enough to be her
father. "The colonel was due to return to England," she
had said, "and it was the only way I could think of to
get home again."

"Was India so bad?" Rose had asked.

"We were in Delhi. It was so hot and dusty. It was a
suffocating world of malicious gossip and long hot
days of boredom." She had lowered her voice to a
whisper. "My dear, I would have married *anyone* just
to get home again."

"Are the Indians so bad?" Rose had asked curiously.

"Oh, *they're* all right. It's the English community
that I could not stand. If there's ever another mutiny, it
will be because of the memsahibs treating them like
dirt."

Harry was thinking about India as well. Why should
I not let this infuriating girl get sent to India? he
thought. Rose has been nothing but trouble. She could
find herself some army officer, have lots of children
and settle down.

Kerridge came back. "I've alerted the Essex police. I
have also telephoned Lord Hadshire to say his daughter
is safe. His lordship wishes you to return immediately."

"I will escort Lady Rose," said Harry.

"Come back here when you've finished," said Kerridge. "I want a word with you in private."

Although he had not believed Rose guilty, Kerridge
was shaken by the discovery of those letters. What if
Rose really had the letters all along and when Harry

burst in on her, she had made up a story about just finding them?

As they approached the earl's town house, Harry said to Rose, "Ignore the press. Just walk past them with your head down."

But there was not even one reporter outside. "That's odd," said Harry. "Let's go in and face your parents."

Rose suddenly clutched his arm and looked pleadingly up into his face. He patted her hand. "It will be all right," he said.

But it was worse than Rose could have imagined. Her father did not shout or bluster. His voice was quiet and decisive. "I have instructed my secretary to send a notice of the termination of your engagement to the newspapers. As for you, miss—"

"I am not going to India."

"No, India will be spared a visit from you. You and Miss Levine are to leave tomorrow for Saint Mary's Convent in Oxford. It is an Anglican convent and the mother superior, Lady Janus, has kindly agreed to take you both for a year and school you in humility and obedience."

Rose looked desperately at Harry. He looked away. He thought that Rose would at least be safe until he solved this murder.

"What if I don't go?" demanded Rose.

"You will obey me, your father, for once in your life."

Daisy slipped out of the room and ran downstairs and out to where Becket was sitting in the motor car. "The earl is sending me and Rose into a convent for a year," said Daisy. "You've got to help me!"

"I didn't know they were Catholics."

"It's an Anglican convent. Look, let's just get married."

"On what? I'm not read yet, Daisy."

Daisy turned on her heel and said over her shoulder. "I'll never forgive you for this."

Rose pleaded throughout the rest of the day in vain. "We could run away again," said Daisy that evening.

"Where to? Harry, Captain Cathcart, would find us and drag us back. I hate that man. He sat there and did nothing. Not one word of protest."

Along the corridor, the earl walked into his wife's bedroom. "Thank God, that's settled," he said, rubbing his chubby little hands. "We won't need to worry about her for a year. We've been too soft on her."

Lady Polly was seated at her dressing table creaming her face. "I was thinking, my dear, that's it's very cold in London, and with Rose gone and in safe hands, we really do not want to stay here. What about Monte Carlo?"

"Great idea. I'll get Jarvis to make the arrangements."

Rose, being undressed for bed by her maid, stiffened as she heard her father's voice raised in song echoing along the corridor outside.

"As I walk along the Bois Bou-long,
With an independent air,

You can hear the girls declare,
'He must be a millionaire';
You can hear them sigh and wish to die,
You can see them wink the other eye
At the man who broke the Bank at Monte Carlo."

She had never felt so alone in all her life.

Daisy read a great number of cheap romances. Unlike Rose, she had comforted herself with the thought that the captain would ride to the rescue. Even when their luggage was loaded into the carriage, even when the carriage moved off, she was sure they would be saved at the last minute.

It was only when the great iron gates of the convent were shut behind them and she saw the stern figure of the mother superior standing on the steps did she realize there was no hope at all and began to cry with noisy abandon.

"Pull yourself together," hissed Rose.

"Welcome," said the mother superior, Lady Janus. "What a great deal of luggage!"

Daisy scrubbed her eyes defiantly with a handkerchief and asked, "Will I have to dress like a bleedin' penguin?"

"I will have to talk to you later, young lady, about your very bad manners. Follow me."

The mother superior led the way along several dark corridors. It was evident to Rose, from what she could see of the architecture, that the convent had been built in the Gothic style in the middle of the last century. She remembered reading that there had been some opposition to Oxford Anglicanism, claiming it was too "high" and drifting back to the Catholic Church.

"You will share a room," said the mother superior, opening a heavy oak door. "As laywomen, you will not wear the habit, but you will select from your luggage your plainest clothes. I will leave you to unpack. Sister Agnes will be your mentor. She will be with you shortly to take you an a tour of the convent and explain your duties to you."

She retreated. Rose and Daisy looked at each other and then around the narrow room. It was furnished with two hard narrow beds. Between the beds was a table on which lay a large Bible. The latticed window let in very little light. Against one wall was a tall narrow wardrobe. "No fireplace," muttered Daisy miserably. "And it's freezing."

"We may as well sort out our clothes and pick out the warmest things we have," said Rose. She looked gloomily at the trunks piled one on top of the other and the hatboxes lying on the floor.

The door opened and a nun stood surveying them. She was dressed in traditional robes. She had a long white face, pale eyes under heavy lids and her thin-lipped mouth was shadowed by a moustache.

"You have far too many clothes. I am Sister Agnes. I will fetch Sister Martha to help you."

When she had closed the door behind her, Rose said urgently, "We must hurry. They may frown on furs, so we must take out two fur coats and hide them under our bedding. We will need them at night or we will freeze."

Rose pulled out a sable coat and hid it under the thin

blankets on one of the beds and Daisy put her precious squirrel coat under the blankets on the other one.

They had just finished when Sister Martha came in. She was small, plump and cheerful. She shook hands with both of them and then helped them pack away the fine dresses, blouses and hats that she considered unsuitable.

When they were finished at last, Sister Martha said, "We'll drag the trunks outside and the oddman will take them down to the storage room in the cellar. We must hurry. We are to go along to dinner. You have missed Vespers but allowances must be made on your first day." She looked uneasily at them. "Do you wish me to retire so that you may change into something more suitable?"

"We will wear what we have on," said Rose firmly. "We are not yet accustomed to the cold of this place."

Sister Agnes looked uneasily at Rose. Rose was wearing a coat trimmed with black Persian lamb and a black Persian lamb hat. Daisy had a frogged military-style coat also trimmed with fur and a sort of shako on her head.

"Very well. Follow me."

The dining room was blessed with a roaring fire. Rose and Daisy were told to take seats at the end of a long refectory table. Grace was said. The food was plain but with generous helpings. The nuns and novices ate in silence. Rose wondered whether they were usually silent or whether the presence of two strangers in their midst had made them shy.

After dinner, Sister Agnes came up to them and bent her head as a signal that they were to follow her. She led them to an austere office and sat down behind a huge desk, indicating two hard chairs in front of it.

"You have been sent here for correction," she began. "You will attend all prayers. The convent owns six homes for fallen women. You will come with me tomorrow. Part of your duty will be to talk to these women and impress on them the folly of their ways.

"The order of your days will be as follows: You will rise at five. Five-twenty to six-fifteen, matins; six-fifteen to six forty-five, private devotions; six forty-five until seven, make beds and clean up rooms; seven to seven-thirty, prime; seven-thirty to eight-thirty, service in church; eight-thirty to eight fifty-five, breakfast; eight fifty-five to nine-ten, terce; nine-ten to twelve-thirty, visiting the poor . . ."

Rose had heard enough. She stood silently while the description of their daily programme went on and on. When Sister Agnes finished with a long lecture to which neither of them paid any attention, she then led them on a bewildering tour of the convent.

When they were finally left alone in their cell-like room, Daisy blurted out, "We'll die here. Why didn't the captain or Becket try to do something to stop this?"

"I don't know," said Rose. "Can you remember where the bathroom is?"

"About a mile to the left," said Daisy and burst into noisy tears.

FOUR

If you become a nun, dear,
A friar I will be.
In any cell you run, dear,
Pray look behind for me.

—JAMES HENRY LEIGH HUNT

Rose awoke with a start the next morning to the sound of a bell. Then she could hear a quick step coming along the corridor as someone knocked sharply at each cell door and called out, "Benidicamus Domino!" Sleepy voices called in return, "Deo gratias!"

When the sharp knocking came at their door and the voice called, "Benedicamus Domino," Rose huddled farther down under the bedclothes and her fur coat covering and pretended not to be there.

"Rose," the voice then called. "It's time to get up."

"Daisy," hissed Rose, leaning across and shaking her. "It's time to get up."

"Shan't."

"We'll miss matins."

I could kill Harry," brooded Rose as they made up their beds. "My knees are already sore with praying."

I could run away, thought Daisy. I kept a bit of the earl's money back. Matthew will have assumed it was money we'd already spent. If Rose won't go, I'll go myself.

Another bell rang, summoning them to breakfast. The banisters outside the chapel were festooned with white aprons, the nuns having taken them off before going into chapel.

The sisters filed in, followed by Rose and Daisy. Each stood behind her seat until the reverend mother had said grace. Breakfast consisted of two thick slices of bread and butter each. Cups in front of each plate were already filled with steaming coffee.

"Where's the sugar?" demanded Daisy.

"Silence!" ordered Sister Agnes. "No sugar and no talking."

The silence was only broken by a nun reading from the Bible in a low voice.

After breakfast, the sisters went about their duties. Sister Agnes said to Rose and Daisy, "You will both meet me in the hall after the service of terce dressed to go out."

The walk to the home for fallen women that Sister Agnes had selected them to visit was just outside the convent walls.

It was a plain Georgian building, which, Rose guessed, had at one time been a private house. The windows, she noticed, were all barred.

Sister Agnes knocked. A curtain at a narrow window twitched and then they could hear the sound of bolts being drawn back and a key turned in the lock.

They entered a stone-flagged hall. Four women

were down on their knees scrubbing the floor. Despite the cold, they were wearing plain blue cotton gowns and aprons and their hair was bound up in blue scarves.

They did not look up and Sister Agnes led Rose and Daisy round them and up the stairs. "We have selected three women for you to counsel. You will impress on them the sin they have brought upon themselves."

She pushed open a door. The women sat on chairs, their heads bowed.

"I will return for you later," said Sister Agnes.

"Thank God, the penguin's gone," said Daisy. "Let's get the introductions over with. I'm Daisy, this here is Rose. Who are you?"

They shyly volunteered their names—Freda, Cissy and Louise. They were in various stages of pregnancy.

"You first, Louise," said Daisy. "What happened?"

"Daisy," said Rose urgently, "we're supposed to be giving them spiritual advice."

"Pooh! Go on, Louise."

She clasped and unclasped her swollen red hands in her lap. Too much scrubbing, thought Rose.

"I was working for a very harsh mistress. She used to beat me. I was a kitchen maid. Then one day, madam said she was going to visit her sister. The master gave the other servants—there were only five of us—the day off but said I had to stay. When they had all gone, he . . . he forced me to pleasure him. It didn't happen again but when I began to show the mistress called me a slut and dragged me round here."

The other two had similar stories. Rose listened in horror.

"But did not the nuns confront the fathers of your children?"

"That's not their way," said Cissy. "The women always get the blame. They work us like slaves and then, after the babies are taken away from us for adoption, the nuns find us places as servants. We either put up with it or we're out on the street."

Their sad stories had taken up most of the rest of the morning. Just before Sister Agnes appeared, Daisy said, "I'm going to give those nuns a piece of my mind."

"Don't," said Rose. "They'll punish you."

"What? That bunch o' crows?"

On the road back, Rose listened with growing apprehension as Daisy sounded off to Sister Agnes about the state of the unmarried mothers.

In the convent, Sister Agnes turned to Rose, "Go to your cell. You, Daisy, come with me."

She marched Daisy up to a wide landing. The community room was on one side and the bakery on the other, and on the wall was a great black crucifix.

"Kneel down and kiss the floor," commanded Sister Agnes.

"No, I won't."

Sister Agnes opened the bakery door. "Sister Monica! Come here."

A large burly nun emerged. "Daisy is in disgrace and refuses to kiss the ground. She must take her penance."

Daisy found herself grabbed by strong arms and her face was thrust down towards the floor. She fought and kicked and struggled but her face was pressed down on the wooden landing.

"Hold her there for an hour," said Sister Agnes calmly.

Daisy wriggled and fought but Sister Monica appeared to be as strong as a stevedore. At last all the fight went out of Daisy and she lay on the floor sobbing. After an hour, she was marched down to the chapel and ordered to pray.

When she was finally allowed to go back to her cell, she found Rose darning socks. Rose listened in horror as Daisy described her punishment.

The usually cocky Daisy looked broken. "Let's try to get out of here," she said.

"I don't think that's a good idea at the moment," said Rose. "They will be watching our every move. I think we should behave like model ladies until their fears are laid to rest. Then, when they feel secure, we shall find a way to leave here."

Daisy began to cry. "Hush," said Rose, hugging her. "We'll find a way."

As the end of March approached, Harry's relief at having Rose somewhere he knew she was safe began to ebb. His brief infatuation for Dolores seemed like a bad dream. He felt guilty at having paraded her at the opera. He had employed a new secretary with impeccable credentials. Her name was Miss Fleming. She was in her forties and worked like a machine. He called on Kerridge periodically, but the man who had followed Rose to Thurby-on-Sea appeared to have disappeared into thin air.

Kerridge said he had contacted the French police

but they had been of no help whatsoever. Dolores Duval's lovers had been very powerful men. But they did volunteer the information that Dolores Duval had left a will, leaving everything to a certain Madame De Peurey.

He wondered more and more how Rose was getting on. He thought she must be furious with him because he had neither received a letter nor a telephone call.

Harry had successfully and profitably wound up several cases. To stop himself from brooding about Rose, he decided to travel to Paris and interrogate this Madame De Peurey.

"Excuse me, sir, are we leaving without seeing Lady Rose? Anglican convents allow visitors," said Becket.

"Good idea," said Harry. "We'll go there tomorrow."

Rose and Daisy had entered into the work routine of the convent. There were to be no more visits to fallen women for them. They worked in the bakery, in the garden and scrubbed and hung out the sheets on washing day.

Conversation was allowed in the bakery, and Rose enjoyed the chatter and the warmth as they helped bake batches of loaves and parcelled them up, as the loaves were destined for various schools owned by the convent, along with the homes for fallen women. Rose was worried about Daisy. She was too quiet and subdued.

The hard work and the routine soothed them and yet they waited for what they thought would be the right time to escape. They both had keys to the earl's town house and planned to slip in and collect Rose's jewels, which she had not been able to take with her.

Daisy had suggested they should go out of London

to sell them to some jeweller who would not ask questions, even if it meant they would not get a very good price.

They were working in the garden, hanging out sheets, when they heard the sound of a motor car's engine. The sound stopped and then they heard the clang on the entry bell.

They both looked at each other in sudden hope. Usually arrivals came by horse and carriage.

Then, after a few moments, they heard the motor car drive off.

"Not them," said Daisy miserably.

"Silence!" commanded Sister Agnes.

How they had talked and talked about escaping, thought Rose, and how each day merged into the next without them doing anything.

The following morning when they were working in the bakery, Sister Agnes came in looking flustered.

"Rose! Daisy! You have a very important visitor. Please present yourself in the mother superior's parlour. No, no, take off your aprons."

They followed Sister Agnes to the parlour. She held open the door for them and then left.

Lady Janus, the mother superior, smiled benignly on them. "Your old friend and a great benefactor of this convent, the Duchess of Warnford, has graciously called." A little lady rose to greet them. She was wrapped in various shawls and scarves. Under her large brimmed hat was a wrinkled, heavily rouged face.

"My dear." She rushed forward and embraced Rose and whispered, "Do as you are told."

Raising her voice, the duchess said, "I heard you

were here and I have asked Lady Janus to permit me to take you to my home for a short stay."

"You are too kind," said Rose.

"Your companion, Miss Levine, will be my guest as well. Now do bustle along and pack your trunks. My footmen will carry them for you when you are ready."

Rose curtsied and left. "What's it all about?" whispered Daisy.

"I neither know nor care," said Rose. "This is our way out of here!"

It seemed to take an age to pack their clothes and then return to the parlour so that the duchess could instruct the footmen to go down to the cellars and bring up their remaining luggage.

At last they were ready. "I wish to have a little word in private with the ladies," said the mother superior.

"I'll wait for you in the motor," said the little duchess cheerfully.

She left and Sister Agnes walked in and stood beside the mother superior. "Rose and Daisy, I have been pleased by your recent behaviour. You must tell Her Grace how well we have looked after you."

A nasty retort trembled on Daisy's lips. As if sensing it, Rose pinched her arm.

She waited but neither Rose nor Daisy said a word.

"You may go," said the mother superior after a long silence.

They hurried out, across the hall and through the open door. It was a mild spring day and birds were singing in the trees.

A highly polished motor car was waiting. A uniformed chauffeur saluted as they approached.

Daisy took a deep breath of fresh air.

"Wait!" They stopped beside the motor as Sister Agnes hurried up to them.

"It was most rude of you not to reply to the mother superior. You will both be disciplined when you return."

"Look, you old crow," snarled Daisy, "buy yourself a razor and shave off your moustache."

As Sister Agnes spluttered in outrage, Rose thrust Daisy into the car, followed her and sat down as the chauffeur shut the door.

They moved off through the iron gates of the convent.

"Now we can be comfortable," said the duchess. "Pooh, you both smell of carbolic."

"It was the only kind of soap in the convent," said Rose. "We weren't allowed to wear scent. We are deeply grateful to you for this invitation. What prompted it?"

"Oh, a friend. No more questions. I must sleep. The sisters do very good work but I find these calls at the convent fatiguing." With that she closed her eyes.

The car purred on out of Oxford. Hot baths with scented soap, thought Rose. No getting up at five in the morning. No more having to sleep in the same room as Daisy. She does snore.

They each sat in silence, not wanting to wake the duchess.

Oxford fell behind as they bowled out into the countryside. They were both warmly wrapped in carriage rugs, and soon Rose and Daisy were asleep as well.

Rose awoke to find the carriage entering a drive through tall iron gates which had been opened by a lodge keeper. They drove slowly under trees. Thick woodland was on either side. Then they passed another lodge and drove through fields where sheep grazed, then under a stable arch and into a circular courtyard.

Looking out at the house, Rose felt a pang of unease. It was a square Georgian building with a porticoed entrance but it was hardly a ducal residence. Was this lady really a duchess? But of course she must be. The mother superior knew her and an impostor would hardly give money to a convent.

"Are we arrived?" The duchess straightened her hat, which had fallen over her eyes.

"Is this your home?" asked Rose.

"No, my dear, only a hunting box. My husband is having extensive building repairs done to our home on the other side of Oxford. I can't stand hammering and dust, so I fled here. Come along."

Rose and Daisy stepped down from the motor. Rose decided to leave questions about why the duchess had rescued them until after they had bathed and changed. Her spirits suddenly plunged. She had so gaily assumed this was a rescue. She had believed somehow that Harry had engineered it. But what if the duchess had heard about them from someone in society and as a do-gooder planned only to give them a few days' holiday? Her father had sworn everyone to secrecy, but servants would gossip. And after Daisy's outburst, Sister Agnes would be dreaming up some nasty punishment for both of them.

She and Daisy were shown to pleasant high-ceilinged rooms. There was a housekeeper and maids to unpack their luggage and footmen to carry up baths. Oh, the bliss of hot water and scented soap. Hot water for baths had been forbidden in the convent.

Then came an efficient lady's maid to help them dress and arrange their hair.

Daisy came tripping in and Rose exclaimed in dismay, "You cannot wear that blouse, Daisy. It's indecent."

"It's all the crack," said Daisy sulkily. "Miss Friendly made it for me."

"I'm surprised at her. We must make a good impression."

Daisy was wearing a "pneumonia blouse," a transparent confection of muslin and lace with next to no collar.

Rose summoned the lady's maid again and Daisy was finally attired in a white lace blouse with a pouched front and a high-boned collar. Rose was wearing a blouse of batiste with a tailored skirt cut on the cross.

She rang the bell and asked the footman who answered its summons to conduct them to the duchess.

As they entered a sunny drawing room, two men got to their feet—Harry and Becket.

"So it *was* you!" said Rose. "I am surprised my parents allowed this."

"They didn't," said Harry. "Lord and Lady Hadshire are in Monte Carlo. I approached Her Grace and she suggested this visit. We called on you yesterday and were met by a nun called Sister Agnes. She told us you were not allowed any visitors and she was so awful that I decided something must be done."

"Visit?" said Rose. "Do you mean we'll have to go back to that awful place?"

"Don't worry," said the duchess, who was sitting in a large armchair by the fire. "Stay as long as you like. I get bored without company, and yet society bores me as well. I hardly ever go to London."

Daisy rushed forward and knelt down by the

duchess and seized one of her hands. "Thank you, oh, thank you," she babbled. "I thought them penguins would be the death of me."

"There, now," said the duchess, looking highly amused. "Don't be too hard on the sisters. They really do good work. But of course, it must be quite frightful if one has not got a vocation. We shall take tea. Please rise, dear girl."

When tea was served, Rose asked Harry if he had found out who had murdered Dolores Duval.

"Every inquiry came to a dead end," said Harry. "I am going to Paris. There is only one other lead. A French lawyer volunteered the information to the police that Miss Duval had left everything to a Madame de Peurey."

"And who is Madame de Peurey?"

"I can tell you that," said the duchess. "Famous grande coquette at one time. Men falling over her. Must be about sixty now."

"She must need the money badly," said Daisy. "I mean, we went once to a home for fallen women run by the convent. Those poor girls!"

"It's not the same for a grande coquette," said the duchess. "She was top of the tree in her profession. Before starting any liaison, her lawyers would meet with the prospective lover's lawyers and a deal would be hammered out. It usually involved a house, servants, carriages and jewels. A clever woman could end up rich."

"At least they can't have children to worry about like those poor fallen women," said Daisy, eyeing the cake stand and wondering if it would be considered greedy if she had yet another.

"But they do. They form a sort of demi-monde dynasty and their children marry the wealthy children of other courtesans."

"I don't know what she can tell us, but Miss Duval must have been fond of her and she may be able to tell us more about everyone Miss Duval knew," said Harry.

"Do take us with you," said Rose. "I've never been to Paris."

"Out of the question. We are not even engaged any more. It would create a scandal."

"Not if I were to take them," said the duchess. "I haven't been in Paris in years. It would amuse me. We shall all go." She rang the bell.

When the butler entered, the duchess said, "Kemp, take a telegram."

The butler went to a writing desk and sat down, pulling a sheet of paper in front of him.

"Let me see; where is Lady Polly?"

"The Palace Hotel in Monte Carlo," said Rose.

"Very good. The telegram is to go to the Countess of Hadshire. Begin. 'Dear Polly, I am taking your daughter, Rose, on an extended vacation as the effects of the convent's discipline have left her with nasty red hands and a spotty face and I do not think you would like to see her looks ruined or her spirits broken besides which she has been consorting with unsuitable company like Fallen Women but do not thank me as it is a pleasure, Yours ever, Effie.'"

The butler scribbled away busily and then said, "If I may be so bold, Your Grace."

"Bold away."

"There is no need to send a long telegram. Telegrams should be brief."

"Indeed. What would you suggest?"

"I am taking your daughter, Rose, on extended vacation. Stop. Convent life ruining looks. Stop. Yours, Effie."

"Nonsense. Too curt. Send mine."

"Very good, Your Grace."

"Am I spotty?" asked Rose.

"No, my dear. But your hands are red. Quite disgraceful. The captain here has been telling me the whole story of the murder of that tart. Fascinating. Quite like a Sherlock Holmes story. It will do me good to be active again. Warnford is driving me mad with his improvements. I have been covered in plaster dust and awakened at dawn by builders erecting scaffolding. Now, do have some more tea. Captain, your man may take tea in the housekeeper's room." Becket rose silently and left. Daisy miserably watched him go. He had not looked at her once.

Holding a thin, fragile china cup and surveying the company with amused eyes, the duchess said, "We shall leave in two days' time. It would be best if we travel to Claridge's and then go on from there." Claridge's Hotel in London was called the home of the motorocracy, the travelling aristocrats, and also used by society ladies who were tired of the strain of catering for a household of guests and preferred to let the famous hotel cater for them.

"Once we get to Paris," said the duchess, raising her lorgnette and surveying Rose's outfit of blouse and skirt, "we must get you some fashionable clothes."

"I would not like to burden you with the expense," said Rose. "We were only allowed to wear our plainest clothes at the convent. We do have plenty of fashion-able items in our luggage."

"Nothing is more fashionable than a Paris gown," retorted the duchess. "Besides, I shall charge anything we buy to your father. My dear Captain Cathcart, do say something. You have been sitting scowling and brooding ever since the ladies arrived. Are you in love with Lady Rose?"

"We are no longer engaged," said Harry.

"That was not the question. Never mind. I must re-tire for a nap. Come, Lady Rose, you must be chaper-oned at all times."

Rose and Daisy retired to Rose's sitting room. "Did you see Becket!" demanded Daisy. "He wouldn't even look at me!"

"You will see plenty of him when we go to Paris," said Rose, "but it is all very uncomfortable, I must ad-mit. The captain went on as if he barely knew me."

"Let's go outside for a walk," urged Daisy. "I want to enjoy this feeling of freedom."

They put on their coats and gloves and pinned hats on their heads and made their way out to the front of the house. "Nothing but trees, lawn and drive," said Rose. "There's probably some sort of garden at the back."

"You know what I think?" asked Daisy.

"No, how can I?"

"I think it's a bit shocking that this here grand house is merely a hunting box. It could house a whole street of people from the East End of London."

"True. But keep such views to yourself or our host-ess will think you a Bolshevik. Ah, here are the gar-dens in front of the terrace."

"And there's the captain," whispered Daisy, "sitting on that bench down by the sundial."

"We should go back," said Rose, suddenly nervous.

As if aware of them, Harry turned round, saw them, and stood up. Rose walked towards him, feeling her heart beginning to thud.

"Lady Rose," he said, "pray join me."

Rose looked over her shoulder but Daisy had disappeared.

Rose and Harry sat down together on the bench. "We are supposed to be chaperoned, Captain Cathcart," said Rose.

"We are in full view of the house and in the open air. The conventions do not apply to the gardens, society obviously never having heard of love in the bushes. Please sit down."

They both sat down on the bench. Rose was wearing one of the huge cartwheel hats which were so fashionable. The crown was decorated with curled grouse feathers. She had her head bent forwards and Harry could not read her expression. He wondered if his remark about love in the bushes had been too crude. What did she think? Was there any passion there, or when he had kissed her, had he been mistaken in what he had considered her enthusiastic response?

At last Rose began to speak. "Captain Harry . . ."

"I think you should just call me Harry. We have known each other for some time."

"Well, Harry, then. I am deeply grateful to you for having rescued us from that convent. How did you manage to persuade the duchess?"

"I had done some work for her. A precious diamond brooch was missing and her household was in an uproar, with one servant accusing the other. I eventually found it caught inside a corset."

"How did you know where to look?"

"I thought it might have fallen down inside her clothes, and the corset, which is not as regularly washed as the other garments, seemed like a good idea. After the convent would not let me see you, Becket informed me that he had read in the local newspaper while he was waiting for me that the duchess was resident at this hunting box. Was life at the convent really so bad?"

"I suppose it would have been all right if I had really wanted to become a nun. The nuns were in the main very pleasant. Sister Agnes was another matter."

"I wish you would not come with me to Paris," said Harry.

"Why?"

"If you remember, some man put those letters in your luggage to incriminate you in a murder. He may appear again."

"If you think he is the culprit, what has it to do with this Madame de Peurey?"

"Miss Duval owned two houses in France. It is possible that Madame de Peurey may have hired someone to kill Dolores, but I will be able to tell better when I meet her."

"I must go with you," said Rose firmly. "The duchess wants to go and I do not want to be returned to the convent."

"I am sure your parents will not approve."

"Is my company so repugnant to you that you will do anything and hope for anything to stop me going?"

"I am only thinking of your safety."

Rose got to her feet. "It is a pity you were not thinking of my safety before you chose to consort with a French whore!"

"I was merely working for her!"

"Pah!"

Rose strode off to the house.

At breakfast the following morning, the butler handed the duchess a telegram. "What now?" she asked. "Oh, it's from Polly. She says, 'Do not approve. Stop. Convent respectable. Stop. Return my daughter immediately. Stop. How are you? Stop. Effie.' "

"Oh, no!" wailed Daisy.

The duchess turned her shrewd little eyes on Rose.

"Is your father High?"

"You mean, High Church?"

"Yes."

"No, the church at our country home, Stacey Court, is Low."

"And does he know these Anglican convents were founded by Edward Bouverie Pusey?"

"No, I don't think so."

Edward Pusey had founded the Anglican convents in the middle of the last century. He was under criticism for being too close to the Catholic Church.

"Good. Kemp, a telegram." She waited until the butler had fetched paper and pen and then she began. " 'Dear Polly. Did you know the sisters were a bunch of Puseyites, all bells and smells and don't think you want Rose there so think it best she comes with me and what were you thinking of to turn her into scrubbing woman really not suitable I am well, Effie.' "

"Do you wish me to insert punctuation, Your Grace?" asked Kemp.

"Send it!"

"My parents may still protest," said Rose uneasily.

"Oh, I think that'll do the trick."

Rose waited uneasily all day. At afternoon tea, she found the duchess in high spirits. "Got a telegram from your ma," she said gleefully. "She says, 'Dear Effie, Had no idea. Stop. Grateful to you. Stop. Daughter unruly so keep tight rein. Stop. Yours Polly.'

"Paris, here we come!"

FIVE

*Alas! If women are going to motor, and motor seriously—
that is to say, use it as a means of locomotion—they must
relinquish the hope of keeping their peach-like bloom.
The best remedy is cold water and a rough towel, and
that not used sparingly, in the morning before they start.
There is one other, the last, but perhaps the hardest con-
cession a woman can make if she is going to motor, and
that is she must wear glasses—not small dainty glasses,
but veritable goggles. They are absolutely necessary both
for comfort and for the preservation of the eyesight; they
are not becoming, but then, as I have tried to point out,
appearance must be sacrificed.*

—LADY JEUNE. *MOTORS AND MOTOR DRIVING* 1902

Daisy was overwhelmed by the grandeur of Claridge's. Lord and Lady Hadshire's homes in London and the country, magnificent as they were, did not
have the same modern luxuries as the hotel, which
boasted electric light, lifts and en suite bathrooms. At
the Hadshires', when she wanted a bath, footmen had
to carry a coffin-shaped bath up the stairs and then fill
it with water brought up from the kitchens.

"It's a world away from the convent," she said.
Daisy, brought up in poverty in the East End of Lon-

don, could never get over marvelling at the vast gulf between rich and poor.

Rose was at that moment allowing the duchess's lady's maid, Benton, to strap her into the long corset which was considered necessary to produce the fashionable S-figure. She was still upset with Harry. She felt sure he had enjoyed a liaison with Dolores Duval. "What would my lady like to wear tonight?" asked Benton.

"You choose something," said Rose.

Benton went to the tall wardrobe and selected a blue chiffon gown embroidered with tiny rosebuds. It was low-cut and the layered chiffon sleeves covered the tops of her arms. All Rose's jewels had been brought over from the town house. "I think the rope of pearls, my lady," said Benson, "Now, the hair."

Rose's long brown hair was piled up on top of her head, pouffed out, and ornamented with little silk rosebuds.

"You look like another girl," said Daisy, who was already dressed and was watching the toilette. "Sister Agnes wouldn't recognize you now."

Rose normally detested wearing a long corset, but for once she did not mind. She felt she needed to be armoured in fashion before she saw Harry again.

"This is a very beautiful gown," said Benton. "Is it one of Mr. Worth's?"

"No, my seamstress, Miss Friendly, designed it and made it for me."

"Then this lady is more than a seamstress!"

Daisy scowled. She was still furious at Becket for having turned down her idea of setting up a salon with Miss Friendly.

At last Rose was ready. She and Daisy descended to the dining room to join the others. Daisy thought it was a shame that Becket could not join them, but in the duchess's eyes he was nothing more than a gentleman's gentleman.

The duchess, already seated at a dining table, flashed and glittered under the weight of diamonds. She had a large diamond tiara on her head, a collar of diamonds around her neck, and diamond brooches pinned haphazardly on her dark blue velvet gown.

"My dear Rose," she said, "how beautiful you look. Don't you think so, Captain?"

"Very fine," said Harry.

"We will have you married off to some dashing French comte, you'll see. Can't you just see our dear Rose on the arm of some handsome Frenchman, Captain?" The duchess's eyes twinkled like her diamonds.

"Alas," said Harry, "I have no imagination."

Had it been left to Harry and Rose, it would have been a silent dinner, but various aristocrats kept interrupting their meal to chat to the duchess.

At last, when the duchess was engaged in another animated conversation with an old friend, Harry whispered to Rose, "Truce."

"What truce?"

"Between us. We cannot go to Paris glaring and staring silently at each other. If it makes you feel any better, I did not have an affair with Miss Duval."

"That means nothing to me!"

"Oh, Rose, please."

Rose sat with her head bowed for a moment. Then she raised her blue eyes and looked into his black ones. "Very well," she said with a little smile. "Truce."

"Thank God for that," chirped Daisy. "All this heavy silence. It was like being back in the convent."

The duchess finished speaking to her friend and turned her attention on Daisy. "Do I detect a certain Cockney accent there, Miss Levine?"

Daisy looked wildly at Rose. "Miss Levine," said Rose repressively, "is a distant relative of mine from a branch of the family which fell on hard times. She has not had my advantages."

"Really?" said the duchess, unabashed. "I had such a business ages ago when Warnford fell for a chorus girl at Daley's. He even had her invited to a house party where she pretended to be a lady. I saw through her little act and sent her packing."

"I do not see what your husband's amours have to do with my companion," said Rose angrily. "Pray talk of something else."

The duchess raised her lorgnette. "You know, animation suits you. You should cultivate it."

The duchess turned her attention to her dinner. She was a messy eater and the front of her gown was soon decorated with the detritus of her meal. Rose, who had been taught to eat ortolans by dissecting them with a sharp knife, wondered what her mother would make of the duchess's table manners as the little duchess picked up the small bird and crammed it in her mouth and then began to pick out the bones.

The pudding was a meringue confection and soon the duchess's gown was liberally sparkling with meringue dust.

"Where shall we stay in Paris?" asked Rose.

"I have reserved a floor at the Crillon. We could

have stayed with an old friend of mine, but I decided it would be as well to keep our mission discreet. Society does gossip so. We should retire now because we need to make an early start."

"How early?"

"We catch the nine-o'clock to Dover. Ladies, wear your motoring gear when we set out."

A *Daily Mail* reporter lurked outside Claridge's the next morning, hoping for some news about celebrities. He saw that someone very important was about to depart. There was the duchess's Daimler and behind it, Harry's Rolls, and behind that, a carriage for the servants. The duchess was travelling accompanied by her lady's maid, two footmen and her butler. The reporter watched as those huge trunks called Noah's Arks were loaded into the back of the motors and into the rumble of the servants' carriage.

He went up to the doorman. "Who's leaving?"

The doorman stared impassively ahead. The reporter pressed a guinea into his hand.

"The Duchess of Warnford," said the doorman. "Her Grace is going to Paris."

"Who goes with her?"

Again that impassive stare. The reporter sighed and fished out another guinea.

"Captain Cathcart, Lady Rose Summer, and Miss Levine."

The reporter grinned. Lady Summer was news. Nobody had heard of her since that murder. He retreated a little way down the street and waited for the party to emerge and began to make notes.

† † †

It was an uncomfortable journey to the station. A gale tore at the ladies' hats and plastered their thick veils against their faces.

At the station, the footmen ran off and returned with porters. They followed their luggage to where it was being loaded onto a private carriage on the train. Daisy was enchanted by the duchess's private carriage, which was like a drawing room on wheels, complete with comfortable armchairs, the latest magazines and vases of fresh flowers.

The servants were told to make their way to a third-class carriage farther down the train, but as Benton, the lady's maid, was to stay with them in the duchess's carriage, Harry requested the company of Becket as well.

Becket tentatively sat down next to Daisy. He felt he could not bear her coldness a moment longer.

"Daisy," he whispered.

"Ye-es?" drawled Daisy in a good imitation of a haughty Mayfair hostess.

"I've been thinking," said Becket. "I was too hasty in turning down your idea of setting up a dress salon."

"You mean it?" said Daisy.

"I'll do the business end, but I don't want to have to serve ladies."

"No, you won't," said Daisy eagerly. "Oh, I'm so glad we're friends again. Miss Friendly will be thrilled. We'll have the most successful dress salon in London."

At that moment, Miss Friendly had just left a lawyer's office in Lincoln's Inn Fields. She stood on the pavement dazed. She had just been informed that her Aunt Harriet, her mother's sister, who had

vowed to have nothing to do with her father ever again
because of his drinking and gambling, had died and
had left her a house in Sussex, jewellery and ten thou-
sand pounds.

Miss Friendly felt bewildered and alone. She
wished she could talk to Rose and Daisy. Then she remembered Phil Marshall, who worked for the captain.
She had met him at a dinner the year before and he had
seemed such an easy-going, sensible man.

She hailed a hack and directed the cabbie to the captain's Chelsea address. Phil stared down at the little figure of the seamstress on the doorstep. He was
practising a haughty air for the day when he hoped to
take over Becket's duties.

"It is I, Miss Friendly," she said timidly.

Phil suddenly smiled. "I didn't recognize you at
first. Come in. You look worried. Is everything all
right?" He led the way into the front parlour.

"Everything is very much all right," said Miss
Friendly, "but I need some advice."

"We'll have a glass of sherry and you can tell me all
about it," said Phil. He poked the fire into a blaze and
then fetched a sherry decanter and two glasses. "Sit by
the fire," he said. "What's happened?"

Miss Friendly took a nervous sip of sherry and told
him about her inheritance.

"You have no more worries," said Phil. "You move
into your aunt's house and you'll never have to work
again."

"It's just that I have this rather terrifying idea.
Daisy—Miss Levine—once suggested that Becket,
Miss Levine and myself should set up a dress salon. I
have a talent for designing and making clothes. Then

Becket said he did not like the idea and I am too timid to take on such an undertaking myself."

Phil sat deep in thought. He was a changed man from the poverty-stricken wreck the captain had rescued. He had thick white hair and a rosy face and kept his figure trim with frequent walks. He admired Miss Friendly. He thought she was all that a lady should be: genteel and shy.

Then he began to wonder and not for the first time if Becket would ever leave the captain. There were times when Phil felt superfluous. He did a certain amount of housekeeping, but there was a woman who came round to do the rough work and it was Becket who answered the door to callers and who drove the captain.

"What we should do," he began and Miss Friendly gave him a shy smile, liking the sound of that precious little word "we." "What we should do is make an appointment with those lawyers and put your proposition to them. You could sell your aunt's house, and with the money buy premises in London. Then you would need to employ, say, two seamstresses to begin with. You'll need a classy name."

Miss Friendly took a sudden gulp of sherry. "It could be an English name," she said in a rush. "Like Marshall and Friendly."

"You mean I could be a partner?"

"You could, couldn't you, Mr. Marshall?"

"I don't really have any money, just a little bit of savings."

"But I have. I would need a manager."

"Bless me!" Phil grinned. "This is so sudden."

"I've thought about it a lot," said Miss Friendly. "It

would be a great deal of initial expense because we
would need to have an opening fashion show."

"Tell you what," said Phil, "give me the name of
those lawyers and I'll make an appointment."

Seagulls wheeled and screamed overheard as the
duchess and her party boarded the *Queen,* which
was to cross the Channel to Calais. "Going to be
rough," said Harry, looking out at the whitecaps of the
waves.

The duchess retired to a cabin as soon as they were
on board. Daisy and Rose stood at the rail and
watched the white cliffs of Dover until a screaming
gale and a bucketing sea drove them back to the shel-
ter of the lounge. Daisy's head ached because the wind
had torn at her large round motoring hat, which was
secured by two large hatpins, and had nearly dragged
it off her head.

Becket and Harry had disappeared somewhere.
Daisy looked at Rose uneasily. "I've never been in for-
eign parts before. What are they like, them
Frenchies?"

"Very like us."

"Have you been to France before?"

"Yes, I went to Deauville once with my parents. Although I must admit all we really met were other English families."

Daisy lowered her voice. "They eat frogs."

"I am sure that's just a story, Daisy."

"I mean, we've been at war with them."

"That was a long time ago. I believe French ladies
are the epitome of chic."

The ferry lurched up one wave and down the next. "I'm going to be sick," moaned Daisy.

"Then we'll need to go out to the rail. Let's get on the leeward side," said Rose. "That is, if there is one."

Rose held Daisy at the rail as her companion was violently ill. Black smoke swirled down from the funnel, enveloping them in a sort of soot-laden fog. Rose tried to persuade Daisy to go back inside, but she held grimly on to the rail, staring down dismally at the heaving grey-green breakers.

Harry appeared behind Rose. "Trouble?"

"Yes, Daisy is seasick."

"She needs brandy. Daisy, for heaven's sake, get out of this gale. I'll fetch you a brandy."

At that moment, the ferry crashed down into the trough of a wave and a great stream of spray dashed into their faces and their feet were soaked because the decks were beginning to run with water.

Rose had always considered herself a new woman, courageous and independent, but she had to admit weakly that it was pleasant to let Harry take over. He fetched brandy for Daisy and then went off and in a very short time had ordered two cabins for them and had the duchess's footmen bring part of their luggage so that they could change.

All Daisy wanted to do was fall on the bunk and go to sleep, but to Rose's relief, Benton, the lady's maid, arrived and took over. Daisy was put into dry clothes and her forehead was bathed with cologne. Then Rose went to her cabin next door and allowed herself to be changed into dry clothes as well. Benton went off to complain to the duchess that two extra ladies to look after was too much and the duchess said sleepily she would hire a lady's maid for them when they got to Paris.

Daisy fell asleep and awoke just as the *Queen* was docking at Calais. She quickly took a small bottle of belladonna out of her case and applied drops to each eye. She had read that belladonna enlarged the pupils and made the eyes look brilliant.

She hurriedly put the bottle away as Rose knocked at the door. "Come along, Daisy. The servants will see to the luggage."

Beautiful words, thought Daisy, thinking of her impoverished upbringing in the East End. Had she ever dreamed that one day she would have ducal servants to look after her?

But as she left the cabin, she found to her horror that she could barely see.

Where's Daisy?" asked Harry, holding out a hand to help Rose alight from the gangplank. "Oh, there she is. What's up with the girl?"

Daisy was stumbling down the gangplank, weaving from side to side, gazing blindly about her.

The ship gave a huge lurch and Daisy went straight over the gangplank and into the water.

"She's being crushed between the ship and the dock," screamed Rose.

But Becket was already running down stone steps cut into the dock. As Daisy surfaced, he leaned out over the water and grabbed a handful of her clothes and dragged her onto the lower steps.

The duchess's footmen nipped down the stairs and helped Becket carry Daisy up.

On the quay, Daisy was promptly sick again, throwing up what looked like a gallon of salt water. The duchess joined Rose. "Drunk, I suppose," she said crossly. "We'll need to stay at the Calais Hotel for the night. What a bore."

Daisy was in disgrace. She was told to stay in her bedroom that evening while the rest had dinner. A tray would be sent up to her.

She picked miserably at her food. She could tell somehow that the duchess felt she had behaved like some low-class creature.

There was a soft knock at the door and she called, "Come in."

Becket entered. "What happened?" he asked.

"If I tell you, promise you won't say anything."

Daisy told him about the belladonna and Becket laughed and laughed until Daisy began to laugh as well.

Finally Becket said, "Were you able to eat anything?"

"Yes, I made a good meal. I like those little birds' legs in garlic butter."

"Those would be frogs' legs."

"What? I've eaten frogs' legs!" Daisy put a handkerchief to her mouth.

"You are not going to be sick," said Becket severely. "There's nothing up with frogs' legs. I had some in the kitchen. You'll need to act like a cosmopolitan lady if we're going to run this salon."

"Oh, Becket," sighed Daisy, lowering the handkerchief. "We're really going to be free at last."

"It's going to be a funny sort of freedom," said Becket. "We'll need to be responsible for our heating and lighting bills, the rent, our food, our clothes—all those things that servants don't need to worry about."

"But we'll be able to get married."

"That's a plus. What about a kiss, Daisy."

They stood up and Daisy put her arms about him. Then they stiffened as they head an autocratic voice coming along the corridor outside. "I'm just going to see if that tiresome companion of yours has recovered."

"Her Grace!" hissed Daisy.

Becket dived under the bed, just as the door opened.

"So how are you?" demanded the duchess.

"Much better, Your Grace."

"I was going to send you back, but Lady Rose told me how brave and courageous you've been in the past. I admire that in a girl. But do try to brace yourself. We leave tomorrow. Be down for breakfast at six. Good night."

"Good night," echoed Daisy.

As the door closed, Becket began to ease himself out from under the bed.

Then, as the door opened again, he slid himself back under the bed.

Harry walked in. He stood in the doorway. "Are you feeling better, Daisy?"

"Yes, thank you, Captain."

"Then we shall see you at breakfast. I assume those are Becket's boots sticking out from under your bed. Come along, Becket."

Becket emerged again, looking sheepish. "We weren't up to anything, sir. Honestly. I came to see if Miss Levine was all right and heard Her Grace approaching and knew it would look bad."

"Don't do it again. You should know better. Follow me."

Daisy scowled when they had left. When she and Becket were married, they could do what they wanted and see each other as much as they wanted, and no amount of expensive meals and pretty clothes could compete with that.

They arrived in Paris at the Gare du Nord the next day and got into carriages to bear them and their mountain of luggage to the Hotel de Crillon. The hotel had originally been the home of the Comte de Crillon and was built by the most famous architect of the day, commissioned by Louis XV. The hotel was seized during the French Revolution and the statue of Louis XV on the Place de la Concorde outside the hotel was pulled down and later replaced by a 3300 B.C. obelisk presented by Sultan Mehmet Ali in 1831.

As they were led up to their suite, Rose glanced in at the salons on the first floor and began to feel like a country cousin for the first time in her life. The ladies were so beautifully gowned and elegant.

Rose was tired after the train journey from Calais and Daisy was feeling exhausted after her adventures. They were both dismayed when the duchess visited them to say she had employed a maid for them and they were to be in their finest, for they were going to dine at Maxim's.

"Why Maxim's?" asked Rose plaintively. "We are tired and hoped to have a simple supper in the rooms."

"Nonsense. Captain Cathcart says that the French lawyer won't give us the direction of this Madame de Peurey. All the famous belles coquettes go to Maxim's.

Someone is bound to have heard of her." She stood aside and ushered a petite little woman into the room. "This is your lady's maid, Odette. We shall all meet in Le Salon des Aigles on the first floor in two hours. But not you, Miss Levine. After your recent adventures, I feel sure that you would be better remaining quietly here."

"She means I'm not good enough," said Daisy when the duchess had retired. "I may as well tell you, Rose, that I have spoken to Becket and we're going to set up that dress salon with Miss Friendly. We're going to get married and we'll be our own bosses."

Rose was dismayed. She realized in that moment how much she relied on Daisy's chirpy company. "I shall miss you," she said. Then she rallied. "Of course I shall buy all my gowns from you."

Odette turned out to have some words of English and Rose had learned enough French from her governess to communicate with her. She felt lowered by the look of dismay on the maid's face as she pulled out gown after gown. "What about the Worth gown?" she asked.

"Too, how you say, out of fashion. But I work quickly." She pulled out a long white satin gown and then a blue one. She opened a large sewing box and got busily to work, cutting and pinning and sewing.

Daisy began to worry. Was Miss Friendly really that good?

As Rose and Daisy watched the little maid working away, they were unaware that Rose had been in the society pages of the *Daily Mail* in London that day, describing her trip to Paris with the duchess and also with her ex-fiancé.

But Harry got the news from Becket and swore under

his breath. Becket had found some English newspapers
in the front hall of the hotel. Harry decided he would
need to be sure that he was with Rose at all times and
that she did not wander off. He knew she had bought a
guidebook to Paris at the station and had voiced a desire to see Notre Dame, among other places.

When he entered Le Salon des Aigles later to meet
the rest of the party, he decided not to tell Rose she had
been featured in the newspaper. She would only worry.
The salon got its name from the medallions depicting
Fortitude, Truth, Wisdom and Abundance, each
flanked by large eagles.

He stood up as Rose entered the room, thinking she
had never looked so beautiful. Her white gown was cut
low and clung to her figure in the new long, soft line.
It was decorated round the neck and down the front
with blue fleurs-de-lis. A collar of pearls set off the
whiteness of her throat, and pearls were woven into
her brown hair. Over one gloved arm, she carried a
ruffled chiffon cape of the same blue as the fleurs-de-
lis. She moved gracefully towards him over the Aubus-
son carpets.

He kissed her gloved hand. "I have never seen you
look so fine," he said.

Rose smiled but reflected she had never felt so uncomfortable. Odette had lashed her tightly into a long
corset and she wished she could escape somewhere
and loosen the ties.

The duchess made her entrance. She was wearing a
grey silk gown laden down with jewels. Again, she had
so many diamonds on her head, her neck and about her
person that Rose wondered how she could even move.

Her jewels sparked fire from the Bohemian crystal objects which decorated the room.

"So we are all present?" said the Duchess. "Good. We're off to Maxim's."

They could have walked because Maxim's also fronted on the Place de la Concorde, but Becket was waiting for them in a newly hired Panhard.

The swing doors of the famous restaurant were held open for them. Hands relieved them of their wraps, although in the case of the duchess it took some time because her diamonds had become caught in her various scarves and stoles.

They made their way past the buffet with its elegant fringe of gilded youth, past the long line of tables to the end of the room, where there was an open space with more tables. A little farther and up two steps, and there was a section set about for dining with a view of the lower floor.

This was where they were to take supper. This is where the best-dressed and wittiest women dined with their male relatives and friends. Down below, a red-coated band was playing waltzes as couples whirled around. The whole restaurant seemed infused with a restless gaiety.

"I do not think any of the ladies dining around us are the type to know someone like Madame de Peurey," said Rose.

"No, they're not. But I see an old friend of mine. I shall wave. Ah, he's coming over."

An elderly roué bent over the duchess's hand, his corsets creaking.

"You look ravishing," he said. "You will take Paris by storm."

The duchess introduced Harry and Rose, naming her elderly admirer as Lord Featherstone.

"Do sit for a minute, Jumbo," she said. "Have some champagne."

"Gladly. I shall feast my eyes on the divinity that is Lady Rose."

"I wouldn't do that, you naughty old thing. The captain here would call you out. I need to find a certain Madame de Peurey.

"Zuzu? That takes me back. What a wonder she was. They fought duels over her."

"And where is she now?"

He cast an anxious glance at a formidable matron at his table. The duchess followed his glance. "I did not know you were married."

"I'm not, yet. Postage-stamp heiress. Widowed. Wants the title and I want her money. I'd better get back."

"Madame de Peurey. She was one of yours for a bit. Where is she?"

"Have you a piece of paper?"

Harry produced a small notebook and pencil. Featherstone scribbled an address. "Right, I'm off. I can feel my postage stamps disappearing by the minute."

"You see?" said the duchess triumphantly. "I knew it would be easy. Now, let's eat."

Rose began to feel light-headed towards the end of the meal. Parisian gaiety frothed around her. Down on the floor, couples swung around in the waltz. The duchess broke off eating to greet old friends who had come up to her table.

"I never thought I knew so many people in Paris," she said cheerfully. "I was sure they must all be dead."

The supper consisted of eight courses. By the time the brandies and petits fours were served, Rose glanced at an elegant bronze clock on the wall. Four in the morning! Lucky Daisy. She would have been asleep for hours.

SIX

The Dowager Duchess carried an air of solid assurance which belonged to a less uneasy age. That slightly raucous note of defiance was absent from her pronouncements. She did not protest; she merely ignored. Nothing unpleasant ever ruffled her serenity, because she simply failed to notice it.

—VITA SACKVILLE-WEST

Two bottles of champagne, seclusion and a magnificent double bed proved to be too much for Daisy and Becket. They were to be married, after all.

Daisy, despite her chorus-girl background, was still a virgin, but as she confided, giggling, to Becket, a dance number where she had to perform the splits five times a night in the past had no doubt eased the way to losing it painlessly.

The gaiety of Paris, the excited feeling that everything goes, had entered into them and they made a happy night of it. Even when Daisy dimly heard the party returning, she did not leap up in alarm but snuggled closer to Becket and closed her eyes in contented sleep.

They set out after lunch on the following day. Rose was delighted to see Daisy look so glowing and happy. Harry, on the other hand, eyed her narrowly, and hoped the wretched girl had not been doing anything she ought not to do.

They cruised along under the budding trees on the Bois, then through a toll gate and out past Neuilly and the Boulevard d'Inkermann to where Madame de Peurey's large house was situated.

It was a large white villa, typical of the outer suburbs of Paris. Becket went ahead and knocked at the door, and when a maid answered it, presented their cards. She disappeared into the villa and returned after a short time. Becket turned round and beckoned to the party that they were to enter.

The maid bobbed curtsies as they entered and then moved to the front of the party and led them through large shady rooms to a garden at the back. Rose expected to meet an elderly woman, still beautiful and elegant, this famous coquette who was reputed to have broken so many hearts.

At first she thought that the round little woman who rose to meet them must be some sort of companion, but she said in a grating voice, "I am Madame de Peurey. To what do I owe the honour of this visit? Pray sit down." She spoke English with a heavy, guttural accent.

They arranged themselves in cane chairs shaded by a vine trellis. Madame de Peurey was dressed in a narrow skirt and a blouse with a high-boned collar over which heavy jowls drooped. Her feet were encased in square-toed boots and she sat with her legs apart.

"As you will have seen from my card," began Harry, "I am a private investigator and I am investigating the murder of Dolores Duval."

"Poor Dolores," sighed Madame de Peurey. "Without me, she would have given it all away. I took her to my lawyers when she embarked on her first liaison. Ah, what a success she was! Then the Baroness Chevenix started to scream that Dolores had stolen her jewels and it was all over *Gil Blas*." *Gil Blas* was a journal which delighted in reporting the scandals of French society. "I advised Dolores to leave France for a little. I told her it was perhaps time she took the unfashionable route of getting married. We do not normally marry," she said calmly. "But with the English milords marrying low creatures like chorus girls, well, I told her she could be a duchess."

"Who were her friends?" asked Harry.

"Just me, I think. The others were jealous of her. She appeared from nowhere some years ago. Poof! Just like that. She told me she was brought up on a farm in Brittany."

"Whereabouts in Brittany?"

"Saint Malo. She said the farm lay just outside."

The air in the garden was becoming unseasonably warm. Madame de Peurey unselfconsciously hitched up her skirt to reveal muscular calves in black stockings.

"I do not wish to appear vulgar," said Harry, "but did Miss Duval leave a significant sum of money?"

"She owned a pleasant villa near here and an apartment in the Sixteenth, and then, on my advice, she invested well in stocks and shares."

Madame de Peurey rang a little silver bell on the table in front of her and when her butler appeared, she ordered tea. "And bring my album."

The duchess, who had remained silent, raised her

lorgnette. "Do you not wish you had led a decent life?"

Madame de Peurey threw back her head in a full-throated laugh. When she had finished laughing, she said, "And where would I be now? Worn out with childbearing and housework? Believe me, I am a success and *you* are impertinent."

The duchess pretended she had not heard the last sentence.

"Ah, here is my album," said Madame de Peurey. "Sit by me, Lady Rose, and I will show you what I was like in the old days."

Rose moved her chair over next to the courtesan and opened the album. There were early photographs of madame riding a white horse in the circus. She had indeed been beautiful, like a plump cherub, all dimples and curls. "That's me with my first, a timber merchant," said Madame de Peurey. "I moved on up the social ladder after him. Now there is me with the next, the Viscount Patrick. Such legs he had! A great catch. And there is the carriage he bought me so that I could drive in the Bois."

Madame de Peurey smelt strongly of a mixture of mothballs and patchouli. Rose longed to move her chair away. Harry came to her rescue. "I would like to see your photographs," he said. "If I might change places with you, Lady Rose?"

Rose gratefully retreated to the chair he had vacated. She wished this odd visit would come to an end. Daisy had fallen asleep, her face turned up to the sunlight filtering through the trellis of vines. Rose watched Harry as he bent his dark head over the photographs and felt a sudden frisson of desire. He looked up at that moment and gave a little half smile. Rose blushed, lowered her head and played with her fan.

Tea arrived. Madame prattled on about her past but they could not find out any significant information about Dolores or why she had been killed. The duchess barely said a word. She considered such persons as Madame de Peurey highly undesirable and so she simply pretended the woman wasn't there. Any qualms she might have had about Rose being in such company were suppressed by her thoughts that her ducal presence was enough to bestow respectability on the flightiest girl.

Back at the hotel, Harry suggested they should travel to St. Malo on the following day. The duchess grumbled, but Rose wanted to go and Rose had to be chaperoned.

The weather was still fine when they set out with Becket at the wheel. Daisy had enjoyed another night of passion and was pleasantly sleepy. They decided to check into a hotel when they arrived at Saint Malo. Dolores had been photographed for a postcard— postcards of famous beauties sold well—and Harry had bought several to show around the town to see if anyone recognized her.

Daisy was disappointed when she found that her room adjoined Rose's and so there would be no chance of a night in Becket's arms.

The following morning, Harry told them all to relax and look around the town while he went off with Becket to see if anyone knew of the farm where Dolores had lived.

Rose and Daisy walked along the ramparts of the fortress town. A steamer advertising Chocolat Meunier lay below them in the harbour, being boarded by tourists.

Daisy was dying to confide in Rose, but decided against it. She felt sure Rose would put down her loss of virginity to her low background.

Harry moved farther and farther out into the countryside, stopping at farms and showing them Dolores's photograph. He was about to give up because the light was failing and he was tired and dusty when he saw a little farmhouse set up on a rise.

He ordered Becket to drive up to it and got stiffly out of the car, his old war wound throbbing.

Harry knocked at the door. A child answered it and stared up at him. Harry, in slow and careful French, asked if he might speak to her father or mother. She was pulled aside by a young woman who demanded to know Harry's business. He showed her the photograph of Dolores. She stared down at it and then jerked her head as a signal that he was to follow her indoors.

A family were seated around a kitchen table having their evening meal. There seemed to be three generations—grandparents, parents and three children. A pot of cassoulet stood in the centre of the table and the kitchen smelt sweet from the bunches of herbs hanging from the rafters. The woman who had called him in explained the reason for his visit and the photograph was passed from one work-worn hand to the other.

When it got to the old man at the head of the table, he said something and Harry caught the name Betty.

He approached him. "Do you recognize this woman?"

"Looks like our Betty," said the old man.

"Your granddaughter?"

"No. She came along out of nowhere one day. In a bad way she was. No shoes. Hungry. We gave her food and then said she could stay if she worked on the farm. Said her name was Betty. That was all."

"Betty?" asked Harry eagerly. "English?"

He shook his grey head. "Betty spoke Breton as well as French. Stayed with us for six months, about. Then one day, we sent her into Saint Malo to buy some cloth and she never returned. We tried to find her. She had called at the mercer's and paid for the cloth and it was there waiting for us. We searched the town but no sign of her."

"She changed her name to Dolores Duval," said Harry. "She was murdered in London."

The family looked at him in shock. Then the grandfather's brows lowered and he said, "Get out of here. Dirty English coming around my home, trying to accuse me of murder."

"I wasn't—"

"Get out or I'll set the dog on you."

Harry walked towards the car. A blue dusk was settling down over the sleepy countryside. The air was redolent of woodsmoke, manure and the ammonia smell of animals. He thought of Rose. He remembered that look she had given him in Madame de Peurey's garden. He suddenly came to a decision. When this case was over, he would ask her to marry him. If she refused, he would never see her again.

The duchess received his news that Dolores had originally been called Betty-something and had disappeared one day on a shopping expedition to Saint Malo.

"This is all becoming rather fatiguing and boring," she complained.

Rose looked at her uneasily. If the duchess became tired of their company so soon, she and Daisy would be returned to the convent.

The hotel was not grand enough for the duchess, although the food was good and the rooms clean.

Rose's worst fears were realized when they set out the next morning for Paris. As she arranged her various shawls and scarves before leaving, the duchess said, "This is all very tiresome. I think I was a bit hasty about that convent. Sterling ladies. Do you good to go back."

"I really think the regime is unnecessarily harsh," pleaded Rose. "Can you not bear with us a little longer? My parents should soon be returning."

The Earl and Countess of Hadshire reclined side by side on deckchairs on the terrace of the Palace Hotel. "Suppose we should be thinking of packing up," said the earl sleepily.

"I've been thinking about that," said Lady Polly. "The Cremonts are going on to Cairo. We've never been to Cairo."

"The Season will be starting soon," her husband pointed out.

"And why should we scamper back for the Season? Rose is in Effie's care and Effie can cope with her. Cairo would be fun, camels and things. I'm really weary of the Season, dressing Rose and parading her around and watching her get into more trouble. Effie can cope."

◆ ◆ ◆

There was a shock waiting for the duchess and her party when they arrived back at the Crillon. There seemed to be a great number of press outside. Magnesium flashes went off in their faces. Waiting for them in the entrance hall was a commissioner of police and two detectives.

The commissioner approached. He looked a little bit like Kerridge with his heavy features and grey hair. He bowed low. "I am Thierry Lemonier. I regret to say I have many questions to ask you."

"About what?" snapped the little duchess. "Come up to my rooms. I am tired and do not wish to stand in the public gaze being interrogated by a bunch of peelers."

"We need to interview your whole party."

"Then follow me," said the duchess and stalked ahead, trailing scarves and stoles.

They arranged themselves in the duchess's private drawing room. Lemonier began. "You visited a certain Madame de Peurey two days ago, did you not?"

"We saw the creature, yes," said the duchess.

Harry interposed. "What's this all about?"

"Madame de Peurey was found yesterday in her garden by her maid. Her throat had been cut."

"Good heavens! Fetch me brandy," said the duchess. She rounded on Rose. "I should never have become involved in your detective exploits. Now look at the mess!"

Harry told Lemonier the reason for their visit, ending up by saying that they had all been in Saint Malo the day before. Lemonier noted down the hotel they had been staying at and then told them he would be grateful if they would remain in Paris.

"But I'm tired of all this," raged the duchess. "I want to go home!"

"Did you see any suspicious persons while you were visiting?" asked Lemonier.

"No," said Harry. "Did her servants not see something?"

"They were going about their duties. Madame de Peurey liked to have a siesta in the garden in the afternoons if the weather was fine. The garden can be easily accessed from the road."

"There was a man on a bicycle," said Daisy suddenly.

"You never said anything," said Rose. "What man?"

"It didn't seem important at the time," said Daisy. "I looked back and there was this man cycling behind us. He was pedalling furiously and I thought he might be trying to race the motor."

"Description?" asked Lemonier.

"I can't say. He had a cap down over his eyes and he was wearing goggles."

"Height?"

"Medium, and he was wearing a grey tweed jacket and knickerbockers."

"Dolores Duval left everything to Madame de Peurey," said Harry. "Perhaps, Mr. Lemonier, you could ask the French lawyer who now inherits."

Lemonier made a note.

"There is something else," said Harry. He told Lemonier about Dolores being originally called Betty and how she had worked on the farm.

"We will interview her lovers," said Lemonier. "Fortunately we know who they are. I shall return tomorrow. I may have more questions for you."

◆ ◆ ◆

When he and his detectives had left, the duchess said angrily, "Go away, the lot of you. I'm tired."

Outside her drawing room, Harry said to Rose, "I am going to telephone Kerridge."

"This is awful," said Rose. Her lip trembled and with a sudden impulse he folded her in his arms. "There now," he said gently. "I will look after you. Go to your rooms and I will join you shortly."

Rose smiled at him tremulously. He pressed her hand and hurried off, leaving Rose looking after him, torn between an odd sort of elation and fear.

But ten minutes later, Becket arrived to say that the captain had been called to police headquarters to discuss the case further.

"Are you going with him?" asked Daisy.

"No, he went off in a police car that was sent for him."

"I feel restless," said Rose, pacing up and down. "Let us go for a walk."

Daisy and Becket exchanged glances. "Do you mind if I stay here?" asked Daisy. "I am very tired."

"Do not worry. I shall go myself, only a little way."

"Becket," said Daisy, "go to Her Grace and ask that one of the footmen accompany Lady Rose."

While he was gone, Rose changed into a blouse, skirt and long coat. Becket seemed to be away a long time and when he returned his normally pale face was flushed. "Her Grace is in a taking," he said. "She said her servants are no longer to be of use to us. It is my opinion she is sulking."

"Oh, I'll go myself," said Rose. "The streets are full of ladies walking on their own."

Rose walked out of the hotel and stood looking at the cars and carriages circling around the Place de la Concorde. She had a sudden impulse to see Notre Dame. She went back into the hotel and asked for directions and then she set out again on foot after refusing the concierge's offer of a carriage.

The concierge picked up the telephone after she had left and dialled police headquarters. He had been told to report on the movements of the duchess's party.

Rose made her way down to the Seine, along the quays of the right bank and then crossed to the left at the Pont Neuf. She walked steadily, enjoying the rare feeling of freedom.

At last she reached Notre Dame and went inside. She sat down in the gloom, dimly lit by all the flickering candles in front of the various saints, and felt at peace.

After half an hour, she left. She felt hungry and had no francs with her to buy food, but was reluctant to return to the hotel.

Rose walked a little way away from the front of the great cathedral and looked down at the river. She walked along to a flight of steps that led to the lower quay. The black water was hypnotic, swirling past. A barge sailed past. She could see the bargeman's family at dinner in a cosy cabin.

She felt a sudden frisson of fear. There was a murderer on the loose in Paris. She should never have gone out for a walk without protection.

She was aware of a movement behind her and half turned round. A man leaped towards her and pushed her violently and Rose hurtled down into the waters of the Seine.

• • •

Harry had gone over and over the little he knew about the case with Lemonier. While he was talking, a policeman came in and handed Lemonier a note.

"Lady Rose has gone out walking to Notre Dame," said Lemonier. "I'm sorry, you were saying . . . ?"

"When? When did she go out?" asked Harry sharply.

"The concierge telephoned about an hour ago."

"Why was I not told sooner?"

"We decided that perhaps you did not want to be disturbed."

Harry said, "I've got to go. She could be in danger."

He hailed one of the new motor cabs and told the cabbie to get to Notre Dame as quickly as possible. Harry fretted as the cab sped over the cobbles of the Place de la Concorde, past the obelisk and down towards the Seine.

When they drew up outside Notre Dame, he hurriedly paid the cabbie and was about to rush into the cathedral when he saw an excited crowd of people farther along looking over the bridge.

He sprinted along and looked down. A figure was struggling in the water. The current was strong. He sprinted towards the steps leading down to the lower quay. He pushed his way through a gesticulating pointing crowd, stripped off his coat and hat and dived in. He didn't know whether it was Rose or not. Harry lunged out and grasped an armful of clothing.

"Rose!" he spluttered, recognizing her. "Hang on."

The great bell of Notre Dame began to ring, booming in their ears, reverberating across the swirling black water.

He struck out for the steps, fighting against the current. Arms reached down to help them and they were dragged up onto the quay. The watchers cheered him as he clutched a dripping-wet and shivering Rose to him.

"Let's get out of here," he said. Someone handed him his coat and hat and he draped his coat around Rose.

A policeman came up and said, "You must come with me."

"Nonsense," said Harry angrily. "The lady will get pneumonia if we do not get her back to her hotel."

"We always arrest attempted suicides."

"I was not attempting suicide," howled Rose. "Someone pushed me."

"You left a letter," said the policeman accusingly. "It is in English, but as you can hear, my English is very good."

"I have just come from Commissioner Lemonier," said Harry. "You will come with us to the Crillon and you may telephone him from there."

Rose was lying in bed. Beside the bed sat a remorseful Daisy. Harry had been furious with her for having let Rose go out alone.

Daisy looked up as Harry and Lemonier entered the room. "How are you?" Harry asked Rose.

"Cold and hot by turns. I am so sorry. I should never have gone out alone. I thought the murderer would have fled somewhere out to the country. There was something about a letter. What letter?"

"This was found on the quay just where you were pushed in. It was weighted down with a stone. I'll read it to you. It says, "I killed Dolores Duval and Madame de Peurey. I do not want to live any more. Rose Summer.""

"I thought I was going to die," said Rose through white lips. "The current was so strong and I felt myself getting weaker and weaker. I called for help but no one seemed to hear me."

"Too busy watching the show," said Harry bitterly. "Monsieur Lemonier, you must know this is rubbish. For a start, Lady Rose was with us in Saint Malo at the time of Madame de Peurey's murder."

"Nonetheless, to be thorough, we will take a copy of milady's handwriting."

"I have a note Lady Rose wrote to me," said Daisy. "I'll get it. No need to bother my poor lady at the moment. You can see she is not well."

Daisy went to her room and found a list of things to be packed Rose had given to Daisy in London and brought it back.

Lemonier read it carefully and compared it with the note. "I have my police combing every hotel and lodging house in Paris, although we have only a vague description. Police are interviewing everyone who was on the quay. Can you remember seeing anyone, milady?"

Rose shook her head. "Funnily enough, just before I was pushed I began to feel afraid and realized how stupid I had been to go out on my own. I did not see anyone. There was no one on the quay when I went down the steps."

Benton, the duchess's lady's maid, came in to see her mistress in a high state of excitement. "You will never believe what has just happened, Your Grace. Lady Rose went out walking beside the Seine and somebody pushed her in! The police are here."

"Will this never end?" demanded the duchess

crossly. "I am no longer amused. We will leave tomorrow, Benton."

"But Your Grace, the police said—"

"Do you think I care what a lot of frog policemen say? My orders are to pack. Fetch Kemp."

When her butler arrived, the duchess said, "Take a telegram. Right. Got paper and pen? Good. 'Dear Polly. Daughter involved in murder and mayhem and whole business is too vulgar for words and can no longer chaperone her so suggest you catch train to Paris and get to the Crillon toute suite and take her away because I have had enough of it. Effie.' Send that right off, Kemp."

But when the telegram arrived at the Palace Hotel in Monte Carlo, Lord and Lady Hadfield were on their way to Cairo and had left no forwarding address.

D aisy rapped on Harry's door during the night and when he answered, she whispered urgently, "Oh, Captain, Rose has a bad fever. She needs a doctor."

"I'll see to it right away."

Harry ordered a doctor to be sent immediately and told the hotel manager also to hire a trained nurse. Then he quietly entered Rose's room. She was tossing and turning and her face was flushed.

Daisy began to cry softly. "I should never have left her."

Harry sat down beside the bed and took Rose's hot hand in his own and held it tightly until the doctor arrived.

Dr. Maurey was an elderly gentleman with silver hair and a gold pince-nez. He sent Harry out of the room while he examined Rose. Harry paced up and down the corridor wondering whether he should wake the duchess. When the doctor called him in, he said he thought Lady Rose was suffering from a severe chill and shock. He had prescribed powders which Miss Levine was to dissolve in water and get the patient to drink every four hours. He would call again in the morning. Harry told him a nurse had been ordered and if the doctor waited a few more minutes, he was sure the nurse would arrive. Rose needed expert care.

Daisy felt useless after the nurse arrived and took over. She wished they were all back in England. The nurse was middle-aged and appeared efficient but could not speak a word of English. Daisy felt so far from home, lost in an alien land. She began to wonder whether God was punishing her for having slept with Becket. What if Becket should decide not to marry her? Daisy had remained a virgin until her affair with Becket, having heard too many stories of girls being seduced and then abandoned.

At nine in the morning, Harry walked along to the duchess's suite to tell her about Rose's illness. The doors were all standing open and he could see hotel servants inside, clearing and cleaning.

"Where is Madame la Duchesse?" he asked.

When he was told she had left early that morning, he muttered, "Selfish old toad."

He went down to see the manager and explained that he would need a lady of reputable standing to act as a chaperone. The manager appeared to find his request as simple as if he had ordered flowers.

Later that afternoon, he introduced Harry to a lady called Madame Bailloux. Madame Bailloux was a small, dainty Frenchwoman in her fifties with small sparkling black eyes. She said she had previously been employed as a companion to the Marquise de Graimont, who had recently died. She had excellent references. Harry told her all about Rose's situation and said that madame would be expected to travel with them to London.

"I know London well," she said in prettily accented English.

"Lady Rose does have a companion, a Miss Levine, but Miss Levine is young and I need someone older to act as chaperone," said Harry.

"I will do my best. I remember seeing Dolores Duval driving her carriage in the Bois," said Madame Bailloux. "Could she not have been the victim of some enraged lover?"

"Then why murder Madame de Peurey?"

"Because Madame de Peurey may have known the identity of this murderer. A time ago, I remember, Dolores Duval was under the protection of a certain Monsieur Thierry Clement. He manufactures cardboard boxes and things. Very rich. I am sure this hotel can furnish you with his direction. Hotels are a mine of information."

Harry made a note of the name, thanked her and said he would arrange accommodation at the hotel for her if she could move in as soon as possible.

He obtained the name of Monsieur Clement's factory and went off with Becket, driving out through the outskirts of Paris towards Roissey. He realized as Becket drove up to the factory that possibly someone as rich as this Monsieur Clement might very well not visit his own factory but leave it all to a manager. So he was pleasantly surprised to be told that Monsieur Clement was in his office.

A small, portly man rose to meet him. "A private investigator," he said in French.

"I am investigating the death of Dolores Duval," began Harry. He told him the whole story and said he was searching into Dolores's background to try to find out who might have wished to kill her.

Monsieur Clement sighed. "Poor Dolores. I was her first. I'll never forget that day. I was walking along the ramparts of Saint Malo and there was this vision coming towards me. She was dressed like a peasant, clogs and Breton coif, but nothing could hide that beauty. I took off my hat and asked, 'What is an angel like you doing here?' She said she was working on a farm. I said such beauty should not be labouring. It sounds very trite now, but her beauty struck me like a thunderbolt. I said, 'Come away with me and you will never have to work again. You will have your own apartment in Paris.'

"She grinned like an urchin and said, 'Very well, I will meet you here in an hour.'

"We had a happy time. Madame de Peurey got her claws into her and the next thing I knew, I had to go to a lawyer's office and sign papers, promising all sorts of things—jewels, a carriage, a better apartment. But a year later, she left me for another wealthy manufacturer, and so it went on. I think Baron Chevenix was the last."

"When you met her in Saint Malo, what name did she give you?"

"Dolores Duval, of course."

"At the farm where she worked, she was known as Betty."

"They have terribly strong accents in Brittany, not to mention their own patois. But once when we were talking of London, she seemed to know it very well. I asked if she was English and she looked alarmed and said she was French."

"Did she have any particular friends?"

"Apart from the terrible Madame de Peurey, no, not while she was with me."

Harry asked him to telephone the Crillon if he could think of anything else.

When he arrived back and went to Rose's room it was to find her fever had broken and she was asleep.

He drew Daisy out of the room and told her about the chaperone.

"I am going to see Lemonier," he said. "I feel the answer to Dolores's murder lies in England."

SEVEN

And (when so sad thou canst not sadder)
Cry;—and upon thy sore loss
Shall shine the traffic of Jacob's ladder
Pitched betwixt Heaven and Charing Cross.

— FRANCIS THOMPSON

Daisy began to feel better as the days passed and Rose regained her strength. Madame Bailloux turned out, not to be the formidable dragon that Daisy had feared, but light-hearted and amusing. She set to teaching Daisy to speak French. She told Rose that the very thing to complete her recovery would be a gown made by the famous French couturier Paul Poiret. Paul Poiret, she said, despised the fashion for light colours. He damned them as "nuances of nymphs' thighs, lilacs, swooning mauves, tender blue hortensias, niles, maizes, straws: all that was soft, washed-out and insipid."

Daisy's romance with Becket had come to an abrupt halt. Harry was out frequently with Becket, travelling to and from police headquarters, hoping all the while that Rose's attacker had been found.

In the evening, Harry and Becket walked up and down outside the front of the hotel, watching the passers-by, looking all the while for anyone sinister. One evening a young man in a tweed jacket and knickerbockers and goggles cycled slowly past, staring at the hotel. Harry and Becket gave chase, halting the cyclist and demanding to know who he was.

He told them rudely to mind their own business. He was English. Harry summoned a policeman and the unfortunate young man was dragged off for interrogation. He turned out to be an Oxford student with impeccable credentials on a cycling holiday.

Lemonier suggested curtly to Harry that he should leave investigating to the French police in future.

As soon as Rose was fully recovered, Harry said they must leave for London. He turned down Madame Bailloux's suggestion that they should wait a further few days until Rose had ordered a Paris gown. The bags, trunks, and hatboxes were all packed. The French lady's maid who had been hired by the duchess had disappeared as soon as the duchess had left.

They took the train to Calais and then embarked on the steamer. Daisy was relieved that the Channel was calm. Then at Dover, another train and carriages to the Earl of Hadshire's town house.

Fortunately, Matthew Jarvis was in residence, along with the housekeeper and staff; Brum, the butler, having gone abroad with the earl and countess. A guest room was prepared for Madame Bailloux.

The first thing Daisy did as soon as she was settled was to go upstairs to Miss Friendly's workroom. It was empty of work basket and material. Only the sewing machine remained.

She rushed to Miss Friendly's bedroom to find it bare, with the bed stripped. Alarmed, Daisy sought out

Matthew and demanded to know what had happened to
Miss Friendly.

"Miss Friendly resigned while you were away," said
Matthew. "She came into an inheritance and has left to
set up a dress salon with Mr. Marshall, who worked for
the captain."

Daisy felt her dreams collapse. What on earth were
she and Becket to do now? But there was worse to come.

I feel we should call a doctor for Miss Levine," said
Rose to Madame Bailloux. "She was very sick this
morning."

Madame Bailloux was crocheting a collar, the cro-
chet hook flashing in and out as she worked steadily.

"That will be because of her pregnancy," she said.

"Nonsense! She can't be pregnant."

"Miss Levine is showing all the signs. Young ladies
when they lose their virginity have a certain air about
them. The expression in the eyes is never the same."

At that moment, Daisy walked in. She looked white-
faced and tired.

"Do sit down, Daisy," said Rose. "I have something
of great importance to ask you."

Daisy sank wearily into a chair. "Go on."

"Are you pregnant?"

Daisy's slightly protuberant green eyes opened to
their widest in shock. "Of course not."

"You are being sick in the mornings, are you not?"
asked Madame Bailloux. "I noticed you have a certain
tendre for Becket."

"I can't be!" wailed Daisy.

"Did you go to bed with him?" asked Madame
Bailloux.

Daisy hung her head.

"Why?" asked Rose.

"Oh, why not," said Daisy defiantly. "We were all ready to set up in business with Miss Friendly. We were to be married. Now we can't. Servants don't marry." Then the burst of defiance left her and she burst into tears.

"Oh, don't cry," said Rose. "We'll think of something."

"I'll have to go to one of those homes for fallen women," sobbed Daisy.

"Nonsense," said Rose. "Out of the question. You will have the baby here."

"And what will my lord and lady say to that when they return?" asked Daisy.

Rose bit her lip.

"If I may make a suggestion," said Madame Bailloux. "Captain Cathcart is not what I would call conventional. I think we must summon him here. It is no use crying again, Miss Levine. Your future must be resolved." She rang the bell and when a footman answered its summons, told him to ask Mr. Jarvis to telephone Captain Cathcart and tell him to come immediately.

While they waited, Rose tried to banish visions of Daisy and Becket from her brain. It was almost impossible for a young Edwardian lady like Rose to envisage such a coupling. Edwardian fashions were a sort of rococo art, shunning the simplicity of nature. Anything approaching nudity was regarded as indelicate. Edwardian décolletage in evening dress was far less daring than in Victorian times, the bosom being veiled with lace or chiffon.

She let out a little sigh of relief when she heard the downstairs door opening and then Harry's tread on the stairs as he mounted them to the drawing room.

"Has anything happened?" he asked anxiously as he walked into the room.

"It has," said Rose, "but nothing to do with the murders. Daisy is pregnant."

"Ah." He studied Daisy, who sat with her head bent for a long moment. "Becket?"

Daisy gulped and nodded.

"I'll get him."

Wicked Paris, thought Daisy, with its effervescent charm, its naughtiness, its seductive air that anything was permissible.

Harry returned, followed by Becket. "Sit down, Becket," he said. "We have a problem. Miss Levine is pregnant."

Becket's normally bland white face went through a series of emotions all the way from shock and dismay to dawning delight. He went and knelt beside Daisy's chair and took her cold hand in his. "We'll find a way," he said.

"As you know," said Harry, "Philip Marshall has left."

"He destroyed our dream," said Daisy. "Becket and me were to start a salon with Miss Friendly. We'd be married and be proper business people."

"That's no longer on the cards," said Harry brutally. "Couldn't you have waited?"

"For how long?" demanded Daisy. "You said me and Becket could get married, but then nothing happened."

"Let me think. You'd better get married as soon as

possible. You and Becket can live with me as a married couple. Then we will try to find some sort of business for you."

"After all Daisy has done for me," said Rose, "I do not think she should have a hole-and-corner wedding. She needs a proper wedding."

"Very well. I think you will find Mr. Jarvis will help you with the arrangements. Tell him to get a special licence. I would suggest, Lady Rose, that it might be a good idea to get the wedding over with before your parents return."

Rose planned a really pretty wedding for Daisy. Miss Friendly was still busy setting up her salon but promised to work day and night to create a wedding gown.

There was the delicate question of whether Daisy should be married in white, but Rose thought the fewer people who knew of Daisy's pregnancy, the better, Madame Bailloux pointing out with French cynicism that she was sure many of the society misses went to the altar already *enceinte*.

Matthew Jarvis had found a quiet City church. Then there was the thorny question of Daisy's family. Daisy was nervous at the thought of her drunken father turning up, but Harry pointed out Daisy could hardly invite her mother and brothers and sisters and exclude her father. Matthew booked the upstairs reception room of a pub near the church.

Daisy's emotions were see-sawing. One moment she was elated about the marriage and the next depressed that she and Becket would still be servants.

• • •

Harry called on Kerridge one day before the wedding. He was touched to learn that Kerridge had received an invitation.

"I've had another communication from the French police today," said Kerridge. "They're no further forwards. Lemonier might be coming over. You see, he feels that Miss Levine may have invented that cyclist and that perhaps Lady Rose really meant to commit suicide."

"Ridiculous!"

"I know, I know. But they are feeling frustrated. Madame de Peurey was in her day a very high-class tart with powerful lovers, and the press are calling the police incompetent."

"I don't really know what to do about Lady Rose," said Harry. "There's this wedding of Daisy's. I kept the announcement out of the newspapers, not wanting to draw any attention to her. Lady Rose mostly keeps indoors. I must think of a way to protect her when this wretched wedding is over."

"I thought you'd be happy about it. I thought you were quite fond of that man of yours."

"Oh, Becket's sterling stuff, but it means I have to give house room to both of them. I'd better find a way to set Becket up in some sort of business. But now that Phil Marshall has left, I'm going to find it very difficult to replace him."

"I didn't think servants were allowed to get married."

"They're not. But I suppose I am considered unconventional enough as it is. Once this wedding is over, I must think of someplace safe to put Lady Rose."

"All this should be her parents' problem, surely," said Kerridge.

"Agreed. But I don't know where they are. I sent a telegram to their hotel in Monte Carlo and paid for a reply. The manager replied saying that Lord and Lady Hadshire had left and he did not have a forwarding address. Where could they have gone?"

"The Cairo season is on," said Kerridge.

"They wouldn't go there. There's a cholera scare."

In spite of the cholera scare, the Cairo season was a big success. No case of cholera had been reported since the beginning of November. Cairo had international hotels with modern luxury and sanitation, very different from the poor quarters of the city. The Delta Barrage, twenty miles from the town, was a popular place for excursions, and some point-to-point races were held there. Military bands played in all the big hotels, and there were dances and social functions every day. Lord and Lady Hadshire declared life in Cairo to be absolutely splendid and were comforted by the thought that Rose was being looked after by the duchess. They never read the newspapers, and their friends who had, did not feel it would be quite the thing to comment on their daughter's exploits. They assumed they knew and pitied them for having such a wayward daughter. Better not to mention it, for having a daughter who had made herself unmarriageable was like—well—talking about cholera.

Rose wanted to ask Daisy what losing her virginity had been like but was constricted by the unwritten laws of society. No young lady should know anything about sex. In fact, an eminent surgeon had just declared that only sluts enjoyed the sexual act. Ladies lay back, thought of England, and suffered.

If it was all so terrible, then what was the point in any woman's getting married and forced to endure years and years of breeding?

She and Daisy were sitting in Rose's sitting room a few day's before the wedding. Daisy was still being sick in the mornings, but rallied amazingly in the afternoons. Rose was stitching wedding garters and Daisy was reading a serial story in *John Bull* magazine.

Daisy was engrossed in the story. It was raining hard outside. The clock ticked on the mantel and a log fell in the hearth.

Rose wished with all her heart she were still working with Harry. The days seemed long and monotonous.

Curiosity at last overcame her. She cleared her throat nervously. "Daisy?"

"Mmm?" Daisy reluctantly marked where she had been reading with one finger and looked up.

"Daisy, what is it like?"

"Getting married?"

"No." Rose blushed. "I mean, what is it like to go to bed with a man?"

Daisy's green eyes shone. "It is wonderful."

"But an eminent surgeon said that ladies are not supposed to enjoy the experience."

"Piffle. If you think I enjoyed it because I am of low class, then you are mistaken. If you love someone, then it is the most wonderful thing in the world."

Rose sat deep in thought. Did she love Harry? He was infuriating. What if he became involved in another case with a beautiful woman? She gave a little sigh. If

Harry really loved her, then he would not have found Dolores attractive at all. And would India really be so bad? She conjured up a picture of a dashing officer kneeling at her feet and proposing marriage.

The day of Daisy's wedding dawned bright and sunny. Hunter, who acted as lady's maid to both Daisy and Rose, exclaimed with delight over the wedding gown. It was made of silk chiffon over silk charmeuse with a beaded and embroidered lace overlay on the bodice and the centre front of the skirt. The bodice and sleeves were edged with beaded trim. It buttoned up the back with tiny silk-covered buttons. On her head Daisy wore a white cloche with a chiffon veil.

Rose felt a lump in her throat when she saw Daisy attired in her wedding finery. She had paid for everything—the gown, the reception and the flowers to decorate the church. Rose was glad she had been left that legacy which enabled her to pay for the wedding arrangements. She was to act as bridesmaid. Her gown was of pink silk with white lace panels and a high-boned lace collar. Her cartwheel hat of Leghorn straw was decorated with large pink silk roses.

Matthew Jarvis entered to say that Captain Cathcart had arrived to take them to the church.

Harry was driving his Rolls, looking very handsome in morning dress. He drove very slowly towards the City, not wanting the ladies' hats to be blown off as they sat in the open car.

"You haven't heard from your family," said Rose. "I do hope they got their invitations."

"I'm sure they'll all be at the church," said Daisy, knowing full well her family had not replied because they could not write and had probably found someone literate to read out the invitation to them. The Hadshire servants had all been invited and were following the car in the earl's carriages.

"Becket still insists he has no family," said Rose. "What is his background? Where does he come from?"

"He never speaks about it," said Daisy. "He talks about having been a soldier once, but that's all and he gets angry if I try to probe further."

Bouquets held in silver holders had gone out of fashion. Daisy carried a spray of lilac and hothouse roses.

The church was a small one off Cheapside. Crowds began to gather on the street outside to watch the wedding party. Harry was best man, so he parked the car and told one of the earl's footmen that he would pay him if he stayed outside the church and guarded it. Then he hurried inside so that he could take his place at the altar with Becket and leave Daisy and Rose to make a slow and stately entrance.

"What's that awful smell?" whispered Becket when Harry joined him at the altar.

Harry was sure the smell was coming from Becket's prospective in-laws, whom he had spotted crowded into a pew. "Must be drains," he whispered back, not wanting to alarm Becket about Daisy's family.

The service was somewhat marred by Daisy's father bawling out the hymns in a loud drunken voice. I wish I had never urged her to invite him, thought Rose miserably. He's drunk already. What's he going to be like at the reception?

But when the service was over and Rose walked down the aisle on Harry's arm behind Daisy and

Becket and heard the bells pealing out and the organ playing, she felt a rush of gladness that despite the drunken singing, everything had gone smoothly.

She had a nervous moment at the reception when Daisy's father, Bert Levine, insisted on making a speech. "I'd like ter say—" he began.

"Sit down, Dad," yelled one of Daisy's small brothers. "You're as pissed as a newt."

The father rumbled round the table to where the offender was sitting and clipped him on the ear. Then he staggered back to the top table. Rose counted Daisy's brothers and sisters: three boys and four girls. Mrs. Levine must have a hard life, she thought. Daisy's mother was a vast woman dressed in a purple velvet gown showing patches of wear.

"As I was sayin'," said Bert, "our little Daisy 'as done us proud. As I was sayin' . . ." He suddenly looked around the room in a dazed way and then slowly keeled over, to be caught by Kerridge just before he hit the floor. Kerridge waved to two of the footmen, who rushed forward and pulled Bert into a corner, where he lay throughout the rest of the wedding breakfast, snoring loudly.

At the end of the proceedings, Daisy, followed by Hunter, retired to the cloakroom to be changed into her going-away clothes. Harry was paying for the honeymoon: two weeks in a grand hotel in Brighton.

They all trooped out to the car and carriages to see Daisy off. Harry took the wheel to drive them to the station. Rose hugged Daisy and whispered, "Come and see me often. I'll miss you so much."

Daisy and Becket got into the car. The guests

cheered. The car moved off. Scruffy children ran after it, shouting, "Hard up! Hard up!" and Becket grinned and tossed pennies to them.

Rose watched until they were out of sight. Then Matthew Jarvis escorted her to one of the earl's carriages. Madame Bailloux and Hunter got in with her. What am I going to do without Daisy? wondered Rose and tried not to cry.

Later that day, Matthew called on her brandishing a telegram. "Lord and Lady Hadshire are returning, my lady. They will be here in two days' time."

When Matthew had left, Madame Bailloux, who was sitting with Rose, said, "I may as well make my preparations to return to Paris. You will not need me any more."

"I am now in need of a companion," said Rose. "Would you consider the position?"

The Frenchwoman wanted very much to return home, but the thought of preserving her savings while she enjoyed free board was too tempting. "If your mama, the countess, agrees, I will stay for a little. Perhaps we should go to a theatre or some amusement tonight to lift the spirits. We have been confined to the house for quite a while."

Rose brightened. "My parents have a box at the opera. We could go there."

"Excellent. I will ask Mr. Jarvis to arrange a carriage for us. We will go *en grande tenue* and then you will feel better, hein?"

The opera was *Rigoletto*. Rose leaned forward in the box, lost in the music. At the interval, Madame Bailloux raised her opera glasses and scanned the boxes, demanding to know the names of all the best-dressed women.

She lowered them and said, "So many people are staring at us. Why is that?"

"I am considered scandalous," said Rose. "They have no doubt read in the newspapers about the events in Paris. I am afraid my parents will really have to send me to India now. I have become unmarriageable."

"The good captain seems taken with you. He is not what I would call conventional."

"I do not think he wants to marry me," said Rose. "We were engaged, but only in name. We arranged it to stop me being sent to India."

"If Captain Cathcart agreed to such a scheme, then he really must care for you."

"I think I irritate him, madame."

"You may call me Celine. We are friends, non?"

"I hope so," said Rose and felt a little of her feeling over the loss of Daisy dissipate.

As they stood outside the opera house after the performance, waiting for their carriage, Rose felt the same frisson of fear she had experienced on the quay in Paris and looked wildly around.

"What is the matter?" asked Celine.

"Just a feeling," said Rose. "I had the same feeling in Paris just before I was pushed in the river." She could see the earl's carriage inching through the press of cars and carriages. Rose scanned the crowd. Apart from the people leaving the opera, there were crowds of onlookers, come to gaze at the fine gowns and jewels of the ladies.

She sighed with relief when at last they were safely in the carriage. "Probably my imagination," she said.

When they arrived at the town house, the first footman told them that Captain Cathcart was waiting for them in the drawing room.

"Don't tell him anything about my fears," said Rose to Celine, as they mounted the stairs. "I do not want to be sent away to anywhere nasty again."

"Why did you go out?" demanded Harry as soon as they walked in.

"I was restless," said Rose. "It is miserable being confined here."

"Someone tried to kill you in Paris and that someone has probably followed us back to London. I wish we knew the real identity of Dolores Duval. I wonder if she was English, but then why would she turn up in Brittany?"

"My parents are due back," said Rose. "What am I to do? They will either send me to India or back to that convent."

"I will discuss matters with them when they return. You must be sent somewhere safe."

"I am dreading their return," said Rose in a small voice. "What if they send Madame Bailloux away?"

"We must see to it that they don't. I wonder if it would not be better to send you out of London before they return." He rang the bell and asked a footman to fetch Matthew. When the secretary arrived, Harry asked, "Can you think of anywhere to send Lady Rose which is far from London?"

Matthew stood for what seemed a long time, his brow furrowed. Then his face cleared. "There is your Aunt Elizabeth."

"She is not really my aunt," said Rose. "She is a distant cousin of my father's."

"Where does she live?" asked Harry.

"In Drumdorn Castle, somewhere in Argyll on the coast."

"Sounds ideal. When did you last see her?"

"Several years ago," said Rose. "Aunt Elizabeth came on a visit to Stacey Court. I remember her as being amiable but eccentric."

"Would you send her a telegram?" asked Harry. "And suggest that Lady Rose goes on a long visit."

"What will Lord Hadshire say?"

"I will deal with him."

Aunt Elizabeth sent a telegram the following day to say she would be delighted to entertain Rose. The day passed in packing and hurried preparations. Rose was to travel north with Madame Bailloux and Hunter, the maid, for company. Harry said he would also send Becket and Daisy up to join her as soon as they had returned from their honeymoon. Rose could only be amazed at how placidly Madame Bailloux accepted all the rush.

It was a long and exhausting journey. First the train to Glasgow and then the hire of a car and chauffeur to take them into the wilds of Argyll over a twisting nightmare road called The Rest and Be Thankful.

Drumdorn Castle was perched on a rocky outcrop overlooking the sea. It was an old castle with smoky stone-flagged rooms downstairs and small cold bedrooms upstairs. Aunt Elizabeth, Lady Carrick, was a widow who greeted them effusively. She was a tall, thin, spare woman, dressed in the clothes of the last century and wearing a white lace cap over grey hair. Her face was wrinkled and she had very heavy, shaggy eyebrows.

"So delighted to see you, my dear," she said. "I do not often have company apart from the servants."

"It is very kind of you to invite us. I feel I should tell you why we have come here."

Aunt Elizabeth's eyes twinkled. "You mean it wasn't for the delights of my company?"

"I am delighted to have a chance to get to know you better," said Rose, "but the fact is, my life is considered to be in danger."

"We do get the newspapers even in as remote a part as this," said Aunt Elizabeth. "I have been following your adventures. You will be safe here. There is a sort of bush telegraph operates in this area. Any stranger within miles of the castle will be spotted. I received a telegram from Captain Cathcart and I gather he is to join us shortly. I find it all very exciting. Do change for dinner and we will talk further."

The dining room was more like a smoke-filled baronial hall. "The wind's in the wrong direction," said Aunt Elizabeth as another cloud of smoke belched out of the enormous fireplace.

Tattered banners hung from the ceiling and dingy suits of armour lined the walls. There was a large landscape painting over the fireplace but it was so black with smoke that it was hard to make out what landscape it was supposed to be portraying.

There was an elderly gentleman in knee breeches sitting on a stool by the fireplace, his white head resting uncomfortably on a caryatid.

"Who is that gentleman?" asked Rose.

"That's Angus," said Aunt Elizabeth. "He was my butler for many years. He doesn't want to be pensioned off and feel useless, so he prefers to remain on duty."

"Are you finished with your soup yet?" demanded a highland footman looming over Rose.

"Yes," said Rose, startled, not yet being used to the democratic freedom of speech of highland servants.

"When you get the warm weather," said Madame Bailloux hopefully, "perhaps the fire will not be necessary." She was sure her gowns would reek of smoke for months to come.

"We sometimes get a few warm days," said Aunt Elizabeth, "but not often."

Madame Bailloux suddenly thought longingly of Paris. The sun would be shining and people would be sitting on the terraces, chatting and drinking coffee. Living in London had been relatively pleasant, but she did not know how long she could take being a guest in this smoky castle.

She sighed with relief when they moved to a drawing room where the fire was modest and did not smoke. The furniture was heavy and Victorian. There were many stuffed birds in glass cases, a grand piano draped in what looked like a Persian carpet, and little tables laden down with framed photographs.

Aunt Elizabeth demanded to be entertained, so Rose sat down at the piano and did her best, although a few of the yellowing keys seemed to be stuck down with damp.

Then the cards were brought out and they played whist for pennies, Aunt Elizabeth gleefully winning every hand.

At last it was time for bed. They collected their bed candles from a table in the hall and walked up the stone stairs to their rooms.

Rose was undressed by Hunter and then climbed into an enormous four-poster bed. It was covered with two large quilts, but the sheets were damp. Rose's last waking thought was that she must get the maids to air them in the morning.

In the following two weeks, while they awaited the arrival of Harry with Becket and Daisy—he had telegrammed to say that he had decided to wait for them—the weather turned fine. Rose, accompanied by Madame Bailloux, went for long walks along the cliffs, fascinated by the many seabirds and the rise and swell of the waves as they crashed at the foot of the cliffs.

She found herself thinking more and more about Harry, wondering if he loved her and wondering if she really loved him. Fear of her assailant had almost disappeared as one sunny day followed another.

Madame Bailloux had recovered her spirits. The fire in the dining room was no longer lit in the evenings, and all her gowns had been sponged and hung out in the fresh air. She chatted away about her beloved Paris and about her late husband, a colonel in the French army, and Rose walked beside her barely listening, thinking of Harry.

At last, the day of Harry's arrival dawned. Rose climbed up to one of the turrets of the castle and looked across the moors, waiting for the fist sign of Harry's car. And there it came at last, mounting a rise in the distance and then heading towards the great iron gates which guarded the estate. The lodge keeper ran out to open the gates.

Rose ran down the stairs and out to the front of the castle. Daisy was the first out of the car, running towards Rose, throwing herself into her arms and crying, "I have missed you."

Rose looked across Daisy's head to Harry. He smiled at her, that rare smile of his which lit up his face, and she felt a surge of gladness.

She extricated herself from Daisy and went up to him. "How are my parents?" she asked.

"At first furious and then resigned."

"Are they coming to join us?"

"Your father says he may come here if you are still here in August. He says one only goes to Scotland to shoot."

Rose's happiness at seeing him was suddenly dimmed. Her parents were moving farther and farther away from her. She knew they now prayed for the day when she would marry someone—anyone—and be out of their care.

Footmen came out to collect the luggage and the housekeeper to take the new guests to their rooms. Rose had had to explain to Aunt Elizabeth that as Daisy had been her former companion, neither she nor her husband could quite be classed as servants and should be accommodated in the guest rooms.

Later, Madame Bailloux went to join Rose in her room but retreated when she heard Rose laughing and chatting with Daisy. She went instead in search of Harry.

"I feel now would be a good time for me to return to France," she said. "Lady Rose has plenty of company."

"Must you? Things have changed now that Daisy is married to my servant. Lady Rose still needs a chaperone."

"But she has her aunt and I would really like to return."

"When?"

"As soon as possible."

At dinner that evening, Harry told the company that
Madame Bailloux would be leaving them.

"Oh, don't go, Celine," exclaimed Rose.

Daisy flashed a jealous look at Madame Bailloux.

"I must go," said Madame Bailloux. "I am, how you
say, homesick. But I will write to you. Now, Captain
Harry, is there any further news?"

"There might be something," said Harry. "The
French police traced an early photograph of Dolores
when she was still working at the farm. It was taken by
a Saint Malo photographer who was struck by her
beauty. Kerridge is getting copies sent to all the newspapers for publication."

"Have you a copy with you?" asked Rose eagerly.

He fished a small photograph out of the inside
pocket of his evening coat and handed it to her. Dolores in peasant dress was photographed sitting on a
stone wall on the ramparts. She was hatless and her
hair was blowing back in the wind.

"Kerridge hopes that there might be some English
connection," said Harry. "You see, that young man who
followed you to the hotel and put the letters in your luggage was English, not French. The photograph will be
published in the newspapers tomorrow and he will let
me know if there are any results. Is there a telephone in
the castle, Lady Carrick?"

"I am afraid not. The nearest telephone is at Inveraray."

"I'll motor there tomorrow. Who is that old man by
the fireplace?"

"That is my old butler, Angus. He did not want to retire."

"I think he's dead," said Harry uneasily.

"Nonsense. He always looks like that."

Harry rose from his seat and went over to Angus. He felt for a pulse and then turned a grave face to Aunt Elizabeth. "I am afraid he really is dead."

Enormous preparations for Angus's funeral were set in motion the next day. Madame Bailloux was urged to stay for it as a mark of respect. She longed to say that as she had not known the man, it was surely not necessary, but at the same time was certain her hostess would be shocked if she said such a thing.

Harry returned late from Inveraray to say no one so far had come forward to say they recognized Dolores.

Daisy and Rose were sucked into the preparations for Angus's funeral. The little church on the estate had to be decorated with greenery, and that task fell to Rose and Daisy.

"Perhaps Becket and I would have fared better in Scotland," said Daisy. "The servants seem to have respect."

"I am sure if you should die, Captain Harry will give you a splendid funeral. Are we supposed to tie large black silk bows at the end of each pew?"

"I think so. I heard some of the servants complaining to Lady Carrick about this business of decorating the church, saying it should only be done for weddings, to which she replied that Angus was now married to God. Rose, could you please ask the captain if he really means to set me and Becket up in a little business?"

"I will ask him today, if the opportunity arises."

• • •

The wake following Angus's funeral seemed destined to go on for at least a week, with everyone from far and wide who had attended drinking copious amounts of whisky.

Madame Bailloux fretted. Her luggage was packed and yet no one was free to take her to the nearest station. She took her problem to Harry.

Harry, feeling that Rose was surely safe, surrounded as she was by so many people, volunteered to run Madame Bailloux over to the Holy Loch, where she could catch a steamer to Gourock and the train to Glasgow. One of the footmen who did not drink was delegated to accompany her all the way to London.

Rose hugged Madame Bailloux and promised to visit her in Paris. She waved them goodbye. "Have you asked him yet?" urged Daisy.

"Not yet," said Rose. "Despite the funeral, Aunt Elizabeth feels it her duty to chaperone me."

As Harry with Becket drove Madame Bailloux off over the heathery hills, Madame Bailloux glanced at one point through her goggles and thought she saw someone crouched, half hidden in the heather, watching them through binoculars. She opened her mouth to say something and then closed it again. Probably a gamekeeper. If she said anything, the captain might turn back and she felt she could not bear another delay.

EIGHT

If a gold ring sticks tight on the finger, and cannot easily be removed, touch it with mercury, and it will become so brittle that a single blow will break it.

— THE HOUSEKEEPER'S RECEIPT BOOK, 1813

At last the long wake was over and the castle fell silent again, apart from the screeching of the wind, for the fine weather had broken and ragged clouds streamed in from the sea. The air was noisy, not only with the shriek of the wind but with the sound of the waves pounding against the cliffs.

To Daisy's distress, Harry had sent a telegram to say that he had decided to go on to London with Madame Bailloux but would return shortly.

"Is it so bad working for him?" asked Rose.

"No, it is just having been your companion, I feel I have now sunk in the ranks. I am a housekeeper, admittedly with light duties. The captain expects Becket to work long hours. He should not have taken him all the way to London. I see you are still wearing your engagement ring on a chain round your neck. Do you keep it there in the hope that the captain will put it back on your finger?"

Rose flushed. "It is an expensive ring and I do not want to risk losing it." She lifted the chain from around her neck, took off the ring and put it on her finger, admiring the way the diamonds flashed in the light of the oil lamp on a table behind her.

Rose sighed and then tugged at the ring. "It won't come off, Daisy. It was always rather tight."

They worked on it with soap and then with oil, but the ring stubbornly refused to move. "You could put a bit of mercury on it and then break it," suggested Daisy.

"I cannot do that! I'll just need to wear it. Yes, Hunter, what is it?"

"The dressing gong has sounded," said the lady's maid.

"Oh dear," sighed Rose. "I am so tired of having to change my clothes six times a day, but Aunt Elizabeth, despite her eccentricity, is a stickler for the conventions. Choose one of the velvets, Hunter, and a shawl. The castle has become so cold."

Dinner was a silent affair. Aunt Elizabeth had periods when she did not feel like talking at all and did not welcome conversation from anyone else.

At least the wind was blowing in the right direction and the great fire kept the room warm.

As the first course was served, Rose felt the hairs rise on the back of her neck. She looked around. Aunt Elizabeth had not hired another butler, and three footmen were on duty to serve the dinner. Rose saw one she had not seen before. He was a youngish man, tall and thin, with a white face, dusty fair hair and blue eyes.

She waited impatiently until they had retired to the

drawing room and asked her hostess, "Who is the new footman?"

"Just some English lad who came looking for work. He has excellent references. He worked for the Countess of Sutherland before this, but his mother in Dunoon fell ill and died, and when he returned to work it was to find he had been replaced."

"I do not know why," said Rose, "but he makes me feel uneasy."

"Now, listen to me," said Aunt Elizabeth. "Young gels are apt to exaggerate. I am sure you lost your footing and fell in the Seine."

"What about the note?"

"Oh, that. Probably some prankster."

"Aunt Elizabeth, two women have been murdered!"

"But what kind of women, hey? Tarts, that's what. And that sort of creature is always getting into trouble."

Rose opened her mouth to argue further, but then decided against it. She feared Aunt Elizabeth might become angry and send her away.

That night, she tossed and turned, wishing the shrieking wind would abate. She wondered about that new footman. He wasn't exactly young, perhaps in his early thirties. But Aunt Elizabeth had said he had good references. If only Harry would return.

She remembered there was a bookcase in the drawing room. The castle did not boast a library. Perhaps it might be a good idea to read herself to sleep. She got out of bed and pulled on a dressing gown, lit her bed candle and went out into the corridor and down the stairs. She began to experience that earlier feeling of unease. Her candle threw great shadows up on the stone walls as the flame streamed in the draught. The fire was still lit in the drawing room. The sound of the wind was less than it was upstairs. She lit an oil lamp, chose a copy of an old favourite, *The Master of Ballantrae,* and settled down in an armchair by the fire to read. After an hour, her eyelids began to droop. She closed the book, extinguished the oil lamp, lit her bed candle again and made her way back upstairs.

When she went into her room, she stiffened. There was a foreign smell in it, a smell of sweat. Rose hurried to Daisy's room and woke her up.

"I want you to come with me, Daisy. I went downstairs to the drawing room to read and while I was away, I think someone entered my room."

"Don't worry. I'm coming." Daisy got out of bed and picked up a brass poker from the fireplace.

They lit all the lamps in Rose's room and looked around. "What made you think someone had been in here?" asked Daisy.

"There was the smell of sweat."

"Can't smell anything. Why would anyone come into your room?"

"I'm worried about that new footman. Remember how those letters were hidden in my luggage? Perhaps someone has tried to hide something incriminating."

Daisy stifled a yawn. "All the trunks and hatboxes are down in the storage room."

"Think, Daisy. If you wanted to hide something, where would you put it?"

"In the wardrobe there, among your clothes. What about your jewel box?"

"It's locked and Hunter has the key."

Daisy longed to go back to bed, but Rose looked so frightened that she said, "I'll look in the wardrobe and you look under your pillows and places like that."

"Nothing here," said Daisy after awhile.

"Try the pockets. Oh, let me."

Rose searched feverishly through the pockets of various costumes and coats. She came to an old tweed coat she often wore when she was walking along the cliffs and plunged her hand into the pocket. Her fingers encountered something hard and smooth. She pulled it out. "Look at this, Daisy!"

It was a necklace of black pearls, smooth and heavy. "Isn't it yours?"

"No. Oh, Daisy, what if it belonged to Dolores? I remember they said certain items of her jewellery had been stolen. Don't you see? Someone is trying to implicate me in the murder again. I'm sure it's that footman. I'd better rouse Aunt Elizabeth."

Aunt Elizabeth was annoyed at being awakened. At first she tried to persuade Rose that it was merely a piece of jewellery she had forgotten about and Rose had pointed out that no woman could forget the possession of a genuine black pearl necklace.

"I am sure it's something to do with that new footman," she said. "Please, please rouse the servants and have him brought here. The police will need to be called."

"Very well. Anything so that we may get back to sleep." Aunt Elizabeth pulled on the bell rope beside her bed. The first to arrive was her lady's maid, Queen.

"Rouse all the servants from their beds and bring them down to the drawing room," ordered Aunt Elizabeth.

They waited until all the servants in various stages of undress had gathered. "Now," began Aunt Elizabeth, "did one of you put a pearl necklace in the pocket of a coat in Lady Rose's wardrobe?"

The head footman, Jamie, stepped forward and said crossly, "We've all been in our beds, my lady."

"Where's that new footman, what's-his-name?"

"Charlie. He's here. Step forward, Charlie."

But Charlie, who had been standing at the back of the group, had disappeared.

Now thoroughly alarmed, Aunt Elizabeth cried, "Search the castle, search the grounds. Get the stable staff up and the keepers and water bailiffs. Get them out on the moors. I want him brought back here. Tell John keeper to ride over to Inveraray and tell the police to come here immediately."

Rose, later looking out of the castle window, saw figures bearing torches streaming out across the moors. Please catch him, she prayed, and let this all be over. Then she worried that Aunt Elizabeth might prove to be like the duchess in Paris and decide she did not like being near someone who caused such upheaval.

Harry, arriving with Becket the following morning, having driven through the night, saw, to his dismay, a policeman standing on guard outside the castle door.

"Now what?" he muttered under his breath.

Becket was too tired to care. He felt he had been unable to spend any proper time with Daisy since their honeymoon.

Harry strode into the castle demanding to know the reason for the police presence. Jamie, the footman, told him they were all in the drawing room and Harry went up the stairs as fast as his bad leg would allow.

A police inspector rose as he entered the room. "I am so glad you are back," said Aunt Elizabeth. "May I present Inspector Macleod. Inspector Macleod, Captain Cathcart." She indicated a portly gentleman seated by the fire. "And this is our Lord Lieutenant, Sir Edwin Godfrey. Sir Edwin, Captain Cathcart."

Harry shook hands with both of them. He smiled at Rose. A shaft of sunlight shone on the ring on her finger. Despite his fatigue, he felt a surge of gladness that she was unharmed and that she was wearing his ring.

Then he turned to the inspector. "What has been happening?"

He listened carefully to the story of the pearls. "But we can't find hair nor hide o' the fellow," ended the inspector. "The policeman in Golspie went up to Dunrobin Castle early this morning and the Countess of Sutherland's butler there said he had never heard of this so-called footman. I believe you have been working on this case."

"Yes, and I have some more news. Dolores Duval was actually Betty Biles, brought up in the East End of London. Her father was English and her mother French. Father, it seems, was a bit of a brute. When Dolores—I will always think of her as Dolores—was fifteen, her father was going to sell her to a local businessman. No question of marriage. The mother had died. Dolores ran away. The father owned a small grocery store. Dolores had taken the money out of the till. She must have gone straight to France. Now, there is a brother, Jeffrey. What did this footman look like?"

Rose gave him a description. "That sounds like the description we had of the brother. No one has seen him for a long time. As he seems to be hell-bent on putting the blame for the murders on Lady Rose, he must have committed them himself."

"But to kill his own sister!" exclaimed Aunt Elizabeth. "Why?"

"As her next of kin, he would inherit unless she had left her money and property to someone else. That is why Madame de Peurey was killed, I think. How he can hope to inherit anything now that we are on to him, I don't know."

"If Lady Rose had not felt there was something wrong with him, he could have stayed and played innocent. I am sure he meant to inform the police anonymously that she had the pearls," said Harry. "And the police might have begun to think it was one coincidence too many."

"I think you had better begin at the beginning," said Inspector Macleod, "and tell me the whole story."

So Harry did, ending up by saying, "That is why Lady Rose is staying here, for her safety."

"I do not think he will dare come near the castle again," said Aunt Elizabeth.

"I will telephone Superintendent Kerridge," said Inspector Macleod. "All the railway stations and ports will need to be watched. I will send the pearls to him by special courier. He will want to send them to the new fingerprint bureau."

"I wonder if he had been in service anywhere," said Harry. "May we ask that head footman of yours, Lady Carrick, and see what he thinks?"

Aunt Elizabeth pulled the bell rope. Jamie, the head

footman, entered immediately. "I've told you not to listen at doors," snapped Aunt Elizabeth.

The footman looked hurt. "I wouldnae dream o' it, my lady."

"Anyway, Jamie, we want your impressions of this footman, Charlie. Did he know his job?"

"Aye, we didnae have to explain duties to him. He'd done it afore."

"That's a good place to start," said Sir Edwin Godfrey. "He sounded English, did he?"

"Aye," said Charlie. "He said his family were Scottish but had moved south when he was a wee lad."

Harry noticed Rose looked shaken. He went quickly to her and took her hand.

"Do not worry," he said. "Now we know who he is and we have a good description, we'll get him now."

She smiled shakily up at him. "I am glad you are wearing my ring," he whispered. Rose somehow could not bring herself to tell him that she was wearing it because she had merely tried it on and could not get it off.

There was a more relaxed air about the castle now that the killer was being hunted down. Surely he could not get away now. The following day, Harry, Daisy and Becket went to Inveraray and Rose telephoned her mother.

Lady Polly was frosty, to say the least. "I am very tired of hearing about your adventures, Rose," she said. "Mrs. Blenkinsop's gel is marrying Sir Peter Winde, handsome and rich. Everyone of your generation is marrying well except you. I hoped that convent would have drilled some manners and modesty into you."

"Mama, I—"

"I want to have a severe talk to you when you return. Your odd relationship with Cathcart has been disastrous. We were in Cairo and the season there is very good. Perhaps next year. Lots of marriageable men, although with your reputation you will probably have to settle for a widower or someone much older. I am very disappointed in you. We had such hopes."

"If that is all you have to say," muttered Rose, "I may as well ring off."

"What?"

"Goodbye."

Rose put down the receiver and emerged from the box brushing tears from her eyes.

"Bad time?" asked Daisy, putting an arm around her shoulders.

"I fear my mother is sadly disappointed in me," said Rose.

"There now. Everything will work out all right, you'll see."

"Trouble?" asked Harry, walking up to them.

"My mother is angry with me," said Rose. "I suppose it is only to be expected."

Becket said, "If you could spare me a few minutes of your time, sir."

"Go ahead," said Rose. "Daisy and I will take a little walk."

"What is it, Becket?" asked Harry as he admired Rose's slim figure as she walked away.

"Captain, me and Daisy were wondering if you could see your way to setting us up in a little business."

"I suppose I must. Can you wait until this case is over?"

"Yes, sir."

"What sort of business?"

"Daisy wanted that dress salon, but that's off the cards now. I wanted a pub, but Daisy really wouldn't like it."

"I often have more work at the detective agency than I can handle," said Harry. "I could extend the business to take in you and Daisy. You both have worked with me on previous cases. Why the long face? Oh, I know. Do not worry. I will find you both a tidy apartment somewhere. Daisy can work a few months and then retire as a married lady before the baby arrives."

"Oh, thank you, sir."

"Then let us rejoin the ladies. I think my ring looks very well on Lady Rose's finger."

"I said I would help them with it later."

"Help them with what?"

"Lady Rose was trying it on and it's stuck on her finger and they can't get it off."

"I should have known," said Harry, half to himself.

Daisy was elated when Becket told her the news about their future. Both were so happy that they failed to notice that Harry appeared to be sunk in gloom and that Rose kept casting anxious little glances in his direction.

When they got back to the castle and Rose and Daisy had retreated upstairs, Rose said fretfully, "I must get this ring off!"

"Why? I happened to notice the captain was quite pleased you were wearing it."

"It's just . . . oh, did you notice how sour he was towards me when we came back from Inveraray?"

"No, I was too happy about working as a detective

and having a little place of our own. Let's go down to the kitchen. Maybe Cook can suggest something."

The cook, Mrs. Burridge, was a thin woman who looked as if she barely ate. "Goose grease is what you need," she said. "I'll warm some up and we'll get to work, my lady."

She heated up a little bowl of the grease and then began to work it gently into Rose's ring finger. Then she pulled hard. There was a *plop!* The ring shot off Rose's finger, skittered and flashed over the stone flags of the kitchen and down a drain in the corner.

"Oh, no," wailed Rose. "I'll never get it back now. Where does that drain go?"

"Down into the castle cesspool, my lady. I am right sorry. I never thought it would just come flying off like that."

"I'll need to tell Captain Harry," said Rose miserably.

She went upstairs and asked a footman to tell the captain to meet her in the morning room. Rose waited nervously, rubbing her sore finger.

Harry came in and stood looking at her. "You sent for me?"

"Yes. I have some very bad news."

"That fellow hasn't come back!"

"No, it's my ring, the one you gave me."

"What about it?" he demanded sharply.

"I was wearing it on a chain round my neck and I decided to try it on. I could not get it off. The cook put some goose grease on it and pulled. It came flying off but it rolled away and went down the kitchen drain and it's now in the cesspool."

"No doubt a fitting burial for it," he said harshly. "Is that all?"

She turned her face away. He went out of the room and slammed the door behind him. He stood with his back to the door, breathing deeply. Then he heard the sounds of weeping and opened the door again. Rose was sitting in a chair by the window. She had her face buried in her hands and was sobbing.

He went quickly across the room and knelt down beside her. "I did not mean to be so cruel," he said. He drew her hands away from her face. Taking out a handkerchief, he mopped her tears. "You see, I had hoped you wanted to wear my ring again."

"I did," said Rose with a gulp.

He drew her to her feet and wrapped his arms around her and turned her face up to his. "Oh, Rose," he said and bent his mouth to kiss her.

"Just what is going on here?" demanded Aunt Elizabeth.

Harry held firmly on to Rose. "Congratulate us. We are to be married."

"No, that you are not. Not without her father's permission. Leave her alone until then. There's a telegram for you." She held it out.

Harry released Rose and took it from her. He read it and swung round to Rose, his eyes shining. "They got him. They caught Jeffrey Biles. You have nothing to fear any more."

"Where did they find him?"

"It doesn't say. I'll go back to Inveraray and phone Kerridge."

"I'll come with you," said Rose.

"Oh, no, you won't, miss," said Aunt Elizabeth. "Not while you're under my care."

"It's all right," said Harry. "I won't be long."

• • •

Rose waited impatiently for the next few hours. At last Harry came back. Rose would have rushed to meet him but Aunt Elizabeth made her wait with Daisy in the drawing room.

He came in and smiled at her. "Jeffrey Biles was arrested at a lodging house in Dumfries. He'd put on a false moustache and a maid at the lodging house caught sight of him gluing it on. She told her mistress, who reported him to the police. Biles tried to say he was doing it for a joke, but the Dumfries police had a description of Jeffrey Biles and so they put him in the cells and contacted Scotland Yard. He's on his way south. He'll be charged first with the murder of his sister and then with the murder of Madame de Peurey. I sent a wire to your parents, Rose, to say we would all be returning to London."

"Lady Rose cannot go with you to London without a chaperone," said Aunt Elizabeth.

"There is Miss Levine," protested Harry, "not to mention her lady's maid."

"Miss Levine is married to your servant and is therefore not a suitable chaperone."

Harry suddenly smiled. "If you want to come with us to London, why not just say so?"

"Well, I would so like to go. I have become used to all the company and excitement."

"Splendid!" said Rose. "But we cannot all fit into your car, Harry."

"I will drive you and Lady Elizabeth and Hunter to Glasgow in a few days' time to catch the London train and then Becket, Daisy and I will follow you by road."

Charlie, the footman, entered the room. "Cook wants a word, my lady."

"Send her in."

Mrs. Burridge came in, followed by a small ragged boy. "Iain here is the pot boy. He said that drain didn't go into the cesspool but in a pipe down into the river. He ran down there and guess what the lad found in the river. Show them, Iain."

The boy triumphantly held up Rose's ring.

"Oh, how wonderful." Rose took the ring from the boy. Harry handed Iain a half-sovereign. "Too much!" exclaimed Aunt Elizabeth, but Iain had seized the coin and scampered off.

Harry took the ring from Rose and solemnly put it onto her finger. "I'll keep it safe this time," said Rose.

The logistics of moving themselves to London proved more complicated than Harry had expected. Aunt Elizabeth had a great deal of luggage. At last, they decided to hire a removal firm from Glasgow to deliver the heaviest trunks to London.

Rose felt happy and carefree on their last night at the castle. Becket played the concertina and Daisy sang music-hall songs, much to the delight of Aunt Elizabeth. The villain was locked up and Rose felt she had nothing more to fear.

NINE

One of the fiercest reform champions addressed a physician, listed all the detriments of fashionable clothing and the threats it posed to health, and said, "Must we wear that stuff? Must we become ill?" The doctor reflected a while and finally said, "Yes, go on and wear it—better a sick woman than an ugly one."

—*THE AGONY OF FASHION*
BY ELINE CANTER CREMERS-VAN DER DOES

London again. Rose felt she had been away for years. After the bustle of arrival, of seeing Aunt Elizabeth settled in her rooms, Rose was summoned by her parents.

Rose's first remark was, "Why, Ma, you are quite brown!"

Lady Polly screeched in horror and rushed to the mirror. "I can't be," she wailed. "I kept under a parasol the whole time we were in Cairo." She turned to her husband. "Am I brown?"

"A trifle," he said. "I wouldn't worry about it. It'll fade."

Daisy, sitting discreetly in a corner of the room, marvelled again at the attitude of Rose's parents. They now knew the perils their daughter had endured, and yet all Lady Polly seemed concerned with was the colour of her skin.

"Lemon juice," muttered Lady Polly. "This is awful. I shall need to make my calls veiled."

She turned reluctantly away from the mirror and faced her daughter. "Well, Rose, we shall need to decide what to do about you. We may as well make use of the Season now you are here. A few discreet calls at first, I think. Good heavens, child, what is that ring doing on your finger?"

Rose braced herself. "I have decided to marry the captain after all."

"Bad connection," said the little earl, reluctantly casting aside the newspaper he had been reading. "Nothing good will come of it except more nasty adventures and scandal in the papers. Give him his ring back."

"I can't," said Rose defiantly. "He could sue me for breach of promise."

"No, he can't. He hasn't got our permission, so there. You are not marrying Cathcart."

As if on cue, Brum announced from the doorway, "Captain Cathcart."

"Look here," said the earl. "You've got no right to creep around behind our backs. You ain't marrying Rose, and that's that."

"I have pointed out to you before," said Harry, "that your daughter has a knack of getting into trouble and she will need someone like me to protect her."

"I have to marry him," said Rose. She threw back her head. "I am carrying his child."

"Oh, Gawd," said Daisy from her corner.

The earl turned puce. "You rat!" he shouted. "I should have you horse-whipped."

Harry tried not to laugh. "Rose," he begged. "This won't answer. Tell them the truth."

Rose's shoulders drooped. "Oh, well," she said. "I tried."

"You mean you're not up the spout?" demanded her father.

"No. But I do think you should let me marry the captain," said Rose. "We could elope. How would you like that?"

"Rose, please," begged Harry. "This is not helping."

"The subject is closed," roared the earl. "Rose, go to your room. You, Captain Cathcart, are not welcome in this house any more."

When the earl and countess were left alone, Lady Polly asked her husband, "What if they do elope?"

"So what? Save us the cost of a wedding."

"But the scandal!"

"Only one more attached to Rose's name. Oh, take her to a few parties and get her mind off Cathcart. There are plenty of respectable men out there."

Upstairs, Rose said goodbye to Daisy again. "I hate leaving you," said Daisy, "but I've got to get back to my husband. I only came with you to see you settled in. Perhaps Aunt Elizabeth can help you."

"Aunt Elizabeth is a stickler for the conventions, but I can try. I'll visit you as often as I can, Daisy. Ask Brum to get you a carriage to take you to Chelsea."

Daisy gave Rose a fierce hug. She went downstairs

and waited in the hall for the carriage to be brought round.

As she climbed into the carriage, she had an odd feeling of being watched. She stood with one foot on the step and looked around. There was a man with a barrel organ at a corner of the square, cranking out wheezy tunes, a nursemaid with a child, a footman walking a dog, but no one sinister-looking.

The house in Chelsea was deserted. She found a note in the room she shared with her husband. Becket had written, "Dear Daisy, Gone out with the captain on a case. Love you."

Daisy felt restless. The rest of the day stretched before her, empty and boring. They should have waited and taken her with them. She was now supposed to be a detective as well.

She took off her hat and went downstairs to the parlour and sat down to read the newspapers. Daisy came across an advertisement for Miss Friendly's salon, announcing the grand opening in a month's time. She took a note of the address and decided to go and visit Miss Friendly.

The salon was in a small shop at the bottom of Hay Hill in Mayfair. Daisy rang the bell and waited. The door was opened by Phil Marshall.

"Come in," cried Phil. "The missus will be glad to see you."

"You're married?"

"Yes, we thought it was the respectable thing to do. Mrs. Marshall is in the workroom."

He led the way up rickety stairs to a room at the top. Miss Friendly—I'll always think of her as that, thought

Daisy—was stitching away at rich material. There were three other seamstresses in the room.

"Miss Levine!" cried Miss Friendly. "How good to see you. How is Lady Rose?"

"Very well, but I am no longer her companion. I am married to Becket."

"How splendid."

"We did plan to start a salon with you," said Daisy severely.

"I know. I am so sorry. But you were not in London and Mr. Marshall was so ready to help."

"It's all right," said Daisy. "Are you getting ready for the big opening?"

"Oh, yes. I do hope you will come. I am going to be very bold. I am introducing a few 'reform' clothes in my collection."

These clothes were the original brainchild of the Reform Movement, which urged women to stop being "lust objects." For a long time they had fought a losing battle against the corset, blaming that argument for every illness from sore throats to corns. Doctors complained that the absence of a corset weakened the muscles. They said, "A good corset is best, a bad corset is bad, no corset is worst."

"Do you think that is wise?" asked Daisy. "These society ladies do not want to be comfortable. They change their clothes six times a day. Maybe they want to be lust objects."

"I am sure some of the more elderly women would welcome freedom from all the constrictions of fashionable dress."

"I saw an interesting gown in Paris for the working girl," said Daisy. "It was a navy-blue tailor-made with a washable blouse and a pleated skirt which showed the wearer's entire foot."

Miss Friendly looked shocked. "Exposing the whole foot! Oh, no, now that would be going too far."

Daisy asked to see some of the collection and spent a pleasant hour before returning to Chelsea. The house was still empty and she wondered what Becket was doing.

Becket was at Scotland Yard with his master, Kerridge having summoned Harry.

"Jeffrey Biles has hanged himself in his cell," said Kerridge.

"Well, that's the end of that," said Harry. "Saves the state a court case."

"That's not what's bothering me. He kept protesting that he had not murdered either his sister or Madame de Peurey. He admitted having gone to see Dolores. He admitted having taken some of her jewels. He admitted the assault on Lady Rose in Paris. So I asked him if he hadn't murdered the women, who had? 'I'm waiting for something,' he said. This was yesterday. 'I'll tell you tomorrow at ten in the morning.' I thought it would probably be a load of rubbish, but I went down to Pentonville Prison this morning, and there he was, hanged and dead as a doornail."

"How had he hanged himself?"

"With a strip he'd torn off his sheets."

"No note?"

"No."

"Odd. I'd like to see the body."

"Why?"

"I'd just like to be sure he hanged himself."

"You're clutching at straws. Case closed."

"Humour me."

"Oh, very well. I'll take you to the morgue myself."

Harry stared down at the dead body laid out on a slab in the mortuary. He regarded the distorted face with distaste. Then he said to the morgue attendant, "Please turn the body over."

"Hurry up," growled Kerridge. "This place gives me the creeps."

The body was turned over. Harry removed his gloves and examined the back of the head. "Didn't you see this?" he asked. "Look here."

Kerridge walked forward. "See the matted hair and blood on the back of his head?" said Harry. "Someone struck him a blow and maybe that someone hanged him."

Kerridge swung round in a fury. "Hasn't the pathologist examined this body?"

"Didn't seem no rush," said the attendant. "Prison doctor signed the death certificate. Suicide."

"I'll get the pathologist to do a proper autopsy," said Kerridge. "We'd better get over to Pentonville and find out if he had any visitors."

But at the prison they were informed that no one had come to see Biles. The warder who had taken him his evening meal said he looked distraught and that he had been crying.

"Where had be been living?" asked Harry when they left the prison.

"Place down the Mile End Road."

"I'd like to go there."

"Why? The room's been cleaned up. The landlord wants to re-let it."

"Just a look."

"Oh, very well. Your man can drive us there."

The landlord reluctantly opened the door of what had been Jeffrey Biles's last address. "Don't go mucking around," he said. "I got someone for this room."

"Mind your manners," snapped Kerridge.

The room was dismal. The dingy window which overlooked the street did not have any curtains. There was a narrow iron bedstead in one corner. A rickety table and one chair stood in the middle of the floor. A small fireplace surmounted by a grimy mirror was against one wall. Beside the fireplace stood a scuttle full of coal and a shovel and poker.

"He might have hidden something," murmured Harry.

"Don't think so. We even looked up the chimney."

"Did you raise the floorboards?"

"Captain, we had our man. And look at the floor-boards. Not obviously haven't any of them been raised in years but neither have they been cleaned in years. I hate the smell in these lice-infested tenements. It sticks to my clothes. Let's go."

"A few minutes."

"Then I'll wait downstairs in the motor with your man. Don't be long."

Harry stood, gazing about him. The roar of the traffic on the Mile End Road reverberated through the little room: the clop of horses' hooves, the growl of brewers' drays, the rumble of omnibuses and the curses of drivers.

He looked thoughtfully at the coal scuttle. Odd to see a scuttle full of coal in such an impoverished room. But Jeffrey had found enough money to go to France and follow them to Scotland. Perhaps he had pawned some of the jewels he had stolen from his sister.

The landlord appeared in the doorway. "Finished?"

"No," said Harry crossly. "Go away. No, wait a minute. I'm surprised you have supplied a full scuttle of coal."

"That was Mr. Biles's. I meant to take it away but the new tenant, he says to leave it, and since no one else wanted to rent a room where a murderer had been living, I had to promise to let him have the coal."

"Good. Go away and don't come back until I call you."

Harry waited until he heard the landlord's feet descending the staircase and then he began to lift the coal out piece by piece and lay it on the floor. At the bottom of the coal scuttle was a tin box.

Harry went to the window and threw it up and called down to Kerridge. "You'd better get up here quickly."

When Kerridge arrived, Harry said, "I've found this box. It was under the coal. I want you as witness when I open it." He wiped the coal dust from his hands with a handkerchief and lifted the box out and took it to the table.

"It's locked," he said. He took out a lock pick and worked away until the lid sprang open.

On top lay a sapphire necklace and a ruby necklace. "Those are the items that were missing from his sister's jewel box," said Kerridge. Harry lifted them out. Underneath were photographs of Jeffrey and his sister, two East End children. There was a photograph of a grocer's shop with a stern-looking man standing in front of it. "That must be the father," said Harry. "Is he dead?"

"Yes, died some time ago."

"And what's this?"

Harry took out a folded piece of paper. He gently unfolded it. In a large round hand was written, "This is the Last Will and Testament of Elizabeth Biles, 19, Sordey Street, Whitechapel. I leave everything I have to my dear brother, Jeffrey." It was signed and dated and witnessed. The date showed that Dolores had probably written it just before she fled to France.

"So there's the motive," said Kerridge. "That would have been legal enough, and with Madame de Peurey out of the way, he could have got the lot."

"I'm puzzled," said Harry. "What did you make of Jeffrey Biles?"

"Weak, frightened—but then a lot of killers are like that after they are caught."

"It's beginning to look as if someone might have faked Jeffrey's suicide. Now, perhaps we have a murderer at large who put Jeffrey up to all this. Say, someone said to him, 'I'll kill your sister and when you inherit, you pay me so much.' "

"Come on. All the evidence is against Jeffrey Biles. He did his damnedest to pin the murders on Lady Rose. He was in his sister's house. He took the letters and he took the jewellery."

"I wonder if he wrote those threatening letters," said Harry, "or if someone else did."

"You're making work for me and there's no need for it. I've wasted enough time on this already," complained Kerridge.

"Humour me. Look, written on the back of this photograph is, 'Me and Betty.' The handwriting looks adult, so he must have written that sometime after the photographs were taken. Why not get some expert to compare it with the handwriting on the threatening letters?"

"Oh, anything for peace and quiet. I'll take this box with me."

"Wait a minute. I want to copy down the names of the witnesses on that will."

Harry wrote down George Briggs, driver, and Sarah Briggs, laundress. "We'll take you back to Scotland Yard first," said Harry.

Kerridge was silent on the drive back. He wished with all his heart that Harry had left well enough alone. His boss would be furious with him. Dolores Duval had been a tart, and that put her in the category of we-don't-care-what-happened-so-long-as-we-can-wrap-up-the-case.

But according to his political beliefs, the lowest in the land were deserving of proper police work just as the highest. He would do what Harry had requested. He insisted Harry follow him to his office to make a statement about finding the box and detailing what it contained.

While Harry was making his statement, Becket went to a phone box and called Daisy.

"Is this what our life is going to be like?" complained Daisy. "I've been mostly alone all day. What have you been doing?"

Becket told her that he had taken Harry to Jeffrey's old address, how he had found a box there and how he had heard Kerridge grumble that Harry did not believe that Jeffrey had committed the murders.

"What does Jeffrey say?" asked Daisy.

"Nothing. He hanged himself in his cell. He was going to tell Kerridge something important this morning, but when Kerridge arrived, he was already dead. The captain doesn't think it's suicide, he thinks it's murder. I'd better go. We'll talk tonight."

"If you ever come home," said Daisy.

Daisy then phoned Rose and told her the latest findings.

"I wish we could do some detecting like we did before," said Rose. "I mean, if Jeffrey didn't do it, who did? I know: If you can find out from Becket the address of that grocer's shop that their father owned, we could start there. I'll tell Mama that we are going down the East End to perform charitable works. She'll agree because she thinks that sort of thing will rehabilitate me in the eyes of society. Come round tomorrow morning."

It was an hour before Harry came out of Scotland Yard and joined Becket. The lamps along the Embankment had been lit and the Thames gleamed an oily black as it slid past on its way to the sea.

"I think we should leave any further investigation until tomorrow," said Harry, much to Becket's relief.

"And where do we go tomorrow?" asked Becket.

"We're going to take a trip to 19, Sordey Street in Whitechapel. Dolores's father had a shop there, or I'm sure he had, because that's an address I found in that box."

As soon as they reached the house in Chelsea, Becket put on an apron and went down to the kitchen to prepare dinner. Daisy had turned out to be a quite dreadful cook. Daisy joined him and gave him a fierce hug.

"Later," said Becket. "We've got to get the captain's dinner ready. I'll grill some lamb chops—that's quick and easy. Thank goodness he likes a simple meal. There's apple pie and cream for dessert."

After he had taken Harry's dinner up to him, Becket laid the kitchen table for himself and Daisy.

"We're going to see that Dolores woman's father, or rather where the father used to have a shop," said Becket, deftly putting lamb chops, vegetables and potatoes on a plate and putting it in front of Daisy.

"And where's that?" asked Daisy. Becket served up his own food and joined her at the table.

"It's in Whitechapel, 19, Sordey Street."

Daisy made a mental note. She decided it would not be wise to tell Becket that Rose meant to go there herself. He would protest and tell the captain and then she would have another day on her own with nothing to do.

"We'll need to ask the captain to get us that apartment," said Daisy. "And you will then need to discuss your hours with him."

"How can I do that? Servants don't get time off, apart from one week a year."

"And I was supposed to work. You must ask him about that."

"I think he is being considerate because of the baby coming."

"But you don't know! Honestly, it's more like you were married to him instead of to me!"

The next morning, after they had left, Daisy took a cab to the earl's residence. Rose was delighted to see her. "I talked to Mama, and she is agreeable. We'd better take a cab so as not to draw attention to ourselves. Your hat is too grand, Daisy. I'll give you a plain one to wear."

Daisy removed her cartwheel straw hat embellished with sprigs of artificial lavender and reluctantly put on a plain straw boater. Rose was wearing a blouse and skirt with a light coat and a broad-brimmed felt hat without any embellishment.

"We must get out before Mama wakes or she will insist on sending footmen with us," said Rose. "This is fun! Quite like old times."

"Rose," said Daisy cautiously, "have you considered that if Jeffrey did not kill his sister and that Frenchwoman, that there might be a murderer out there?"

"I should be safe," said Rose. "Say it is someone else who was manipulating Jeffrey into trying to put the blame on me, well, now, as far as he knows, he has a scapegoat in the late Jeffrey."

"Still, he might be dangerous," said Daisy. "I mean, if he murdered Jeffrey, how did he manage to do it?"

"Some visitor?"

"I asked Becket and he asked the captain last night after dinner. The captain said that no one was logged in the prison book."

"Odd. But let's go."

• • •

Harry arrived at 19, Sordey Street. It was still a grocer's shop, a small dingy place. He opened the door and a bell tied by a rope above the door clanged loudly. A woman was behind the counter, slapping butter into blocks with two wooden paddles.

"Can I 'elp you?" she asked.

She was a tall, thin woman with a lantern-jawed face and her hair tied tightly in a scarlet kerchief. The type of woman, Harry thought, who might have knitted below the scaffold during the French Revolution.

"I believe a Mr. Biles used to own this shop," he said.

"So what's that to you?"

Harry presented his card. She squinted at it and then glared at him. "We don't like nosy parkers round 'ere."

"It's a simple question. Did a Mr. Biles own this shop?"

"If you're not buying anythink, shove off."

Rose and Daisy saw Becket's car outside the shop and told the driver to go farther along the street. "We'll wait until they've gone," said Rose. "I think Harry would send me home if he saw me."

Rose peered out the small back window. "Harry's come out. He looks angry. I don't think he got anywhere."

"They don't trust people asking questions around here," said Daisy, feeling confident now that she was back in her home ground of London's East End. "I tell you what. When we go in, you don't say anything. Leave the talking to me. We'd better buy a lot of stuff. I bet they never thought of that."

They waited until they saw them drive off. Telling the

cabbie to wait, they made their way back to the shop.

Daisy smiled brightly at the woman behind the counter and her voice changed back to its old Cockney accent as she asked, "Got any ham, luv?"

"Fine bit o' Wiltshire."

"I'll take a pound o' that."

"A pound!" The woman's grim features lightened. She heaved a ham onto the slicing machine. "You're not from around here?"

"Used ter be," chirped Daisy. "I was in the chorus at Butler's."

"Was you now? I used ter go there Saturday nights. Luvverley it was."

"I'm down visiting me family. I'll take a pound of butter as well. I know everywhere around 'ere. Hey, wasn't there a grumpy man who used to own this shop? Can't remember his name. Oh, a pound of sugar as well."

"That ud be Biles. Died o' a heart attack. The son sold the shop to me." She lowered her voice. "The son, Jeffrey, been banged up for murder."

"Never!" screeched Daisy.

"Yus. Murdered his own sister."

"Did you know the sister?"

"Member her, way back. Pretty little thing. Ran away. He used to beat 'er. He wanted 'er to go with Mr. Jones, him what owned the haberdashery down the Mile End Road. Lived in Breem Lane. Now, she was but fifteen and Jones was in 'is late thirties. Scandal, it were. Betty, that was the daughter, she said she wouldn't and Biles beat the living daylights out of her. She took the money out of the till and just went off. Can't say I blame her."

"I'm sure this Mr. Jones found someone else."

"Yes, he got himself a nice little bride and it all worked out in the end."

Daisy paid for the groceries and they left and walked back to the waiting cab. "That ham did not look fresh," said Rose. "Give it away."

"If I give it away to someone nearby, word'll get back to her. Let's find out where Breem Lane is."

Breem Lane was narrow and dirty. Scruffy children without shoes played in the dirt. Blowsy women hung out of windows and stared at the carriage.

"Better let me go on with the talking," said Daisy as they both stood uneasily by the cab.

She shouted up to a fat woman at one of the windows, "Mr. Jones, the haberdasher, live here?"

"Naw, left to go live uptown."

"Where would that be?"

The woman half turned her head and shouted, "Marigold!"

"What is it, Ma?" a voice called from inside the flat.

"Someone wanting Jones's address. 'Member, him what 'ad the haberdashery."

"Notting Hill it were. Chepstow Mansions. Real posh. Liza went to do the cleaning once, but they got rid o' her."

Daisy thanked the woman. They got back in the cab. "Notting Hill," Daisy shouted up to the driver. "Chepstow Mansions."

"You're running up a fearsome bill," grumbled the cabby.

"Get on with you," ordered Daisy. "We've got the money."

She lowered the trap in the roof and sank back next

to Rose. "You have got the money, I hope," said Daisy.

"Yes, I came prepared. Oh, wait. Look at that poor woman. I don't think she's had a meal in ages." Rose rapped on the roof with her parasol and the cab came to a halt.

"Give her the groceries," said Rose.

Daisy got out of the cab and handed the woman the paper bags full of groceries and then quickly got back in again. "Drive on," she shouted.

Meanwhile, Harry and Becket had spent a weary time looking for the witnesses, George and Sarah Briggs. No one seemed to have heard of them. But people regarded them with suspicion.

At last, Becket cleared his throat and said cautiously, "You might try offering money for information, sir. If I were you, I would start with one shilling and a bright child."

"I think we're attracting too much attention with this motor. Drive off and park it somewhere up in the City and then we'll take a cab and when we get back here, we'll walk about on foot."

When they returned to Sordey Street, Harry spotted a child who could have posed for an illustration of the Artful Dodger. He was lounging against a lamp post, his hands in his pockets.

"Would you like to earn some money?" asked Harry.

"What for?"

"Information. I'm trying to find a Mr. George Briggs, a driver."

The boy took off his battered hat and stared thoughtfully inside as if consulting the oracle. "How much, guv?"

"One shilling."

"Garn."

"Oh, all right. Half a crown."

"Let's see the money."

Harry took out half a crown and handed it to him. The boy crammed his hat on his head. He put the half crown in his jacket pocket. Then he grinned at them.

"Dunno," he said and ran off as fast as his legs could carry him.

But two other boys had witnessed the transaction. One stepped forward. "We can find old Briggs for you. But it'll be half a crown each."

"No tricks," said Harry. "You don't get a penny until you take us to him."

The boys set off and Harry and Becket followed. They walked through one miserable street after another. The weather had turned warm and humid. The air was redolent with all the smells of dirt and poverty.

"We must set up a charitable trust for these sort of people now that we are in funds," said Harry. All the money he had earned he had invested shrewdly.

"If I may be so bold, sir," said Becket crossly, "charity begins at home."

"Meaning?"

"Meaning me and Daisy would like that little apartment."

"You are quite a nag, Becket. I'll see to it."

"Up there," said one of the boys, coming to a halt. He pointed up at a tenement.

"No money until I know he's there. Which floor?"

"Up the top."

"Then follow us."

Harry climbed the stairs to the top of the ramshackle building. "That door," said the other boy, pointing.

Harry knocked. He heard the sound of slow, shuffling footsteps and then the door opened.

A stooped, grey-haired man opened the door. "Mr. George Briggs?" asked Harry.

"Yes, who wants ter know?"

Harry gave a crown to the boys and said, "Run along with you."

Then he faced George Briggs. "May we come in?"

"You're not from the police?"

"No."

"Come in, then."

The flat consisted of one room with a bed set into a recess. Briggs sank into a battered armchair. "What's this about?"

"Do you remember Betty Biles?"

"Course I do. Prettiest thing to ever grow out o' this muck heap."

"You and your wife witnessed a will she wrote."

"I'd forgot about that. She come round here with her brother and she was black and blue. Old Biles had taken 'is belt to her cos she wouldn't marry Tim Jones. She said she was running away and she was going to be rich and she wanted to make sure anything she got would go to the brother, Jeffrey."

Harry told him the story of Dolores's murder. "Poor soul," said Briggs. "I 'eard about that. Fancy her brother doing it! They were that close."

"Jeffrey has hanged himself," said Harry. "If there is a chance he did not do the murder, who would?"

"Blessed if I know. The only nasty piece o' work in that girl's life was her father."

"What about this Tim Jones?"

"Oh, him. He got a haberdashery down the Mile End Road. But I heard he'd sold it and moved uptown."

"You don't know where?"

"Haven't a clue."

"What about your wife? Would she know?"

"My Sarah's been dead this past five years. But you could try round Breem Lane, where he used to live. Maybe someone there would know."

The fat woman in Breem Lane shouted down to Harry and Becket. "Everyone wants to find Jones today. There was two young ladies asking. Come in a cab."

"What were they like?" asked Harry.

"There was a cheeky Cockney one and the other was pretty but didn't say a word. I told 'em Jones had moved up to Notting Hill—Chepstow Mansions."

"That must be Rose and Daisy," said Harry. "We'll need to hurry." He called back up to the woman, "When was this?"

"Must ha' been a couple o' hours ago."

"Let's go," said Harry urgently. "They could be in danger."

TEN

Come away; poverty's catching

—APHRA BEHN

Rose and Daisy located Chepstow Mansions. It was a new building of red brick off the Portobello Road.

"He must have done well out of the sale of his shop to move all the way here," said Rose.

Inside the hall of the flats, a porter was on duty. Rose asked for Mr. Jones. "He won't be in at the moment, ladies," said the porter. "You'll find him at his shop. You can't miss it. It's right on the cross."

They paid off the cabbie and walked up to the cross and there it was: Jones Haberdashery, a double-fronted shop.

"Looks prosperous," said Rose. "Let's go in."

"I'm hungry," complained Daisy.

"We'll eat as soon as we've seen him."

Rose pushed opened the door of the shop and Daisy followed her in. A stout women in a black dress approached them. "We are just about to close."

"We've come to see Mr. Jones. Here is my card."

The woman took Rose's card and retreated into the back shop. She returned after a few moments, looking flustered. "I am afraid Mr. Jones has left for the night."

"I'm sure he's in there," said Rose when they walked outside.

"You went the wrong way about it. We should have asked about ribbons or something."

"If he's an innocent man, the sight of my name wouldn't frighten him. Oh, look, there's a tea room across the road. We can have something to eat and drink and watch and see if he leaves."

They ordered tea and buttered muffins and sat at a table in the bay of the window. A boy came out and started to put shutters up over the windows. After some time, the woman who had spoken to them left with two other women.

They waited and waited. "I wonder if there's a back door," said Rose uneasily.

"Come on," said Daisy. "We'd better go and look. Can't sit here all night."

A narrow lane ran up the side of the shop. This led to another lane along the back of the shops.

"He must have left from the back," sighed Rose. "Let's go back to Chepstow Mansions and try him there."

But the first thing they saw as they approached the block of flats was Harry's car parked outside.

"They've beaten us to it," mourned Daisy. "We may as well wait for them and get them to drive us home."

They both leaned against the car.

A policeman approached them and eyed them up and down. "Now, now," he said. "Go about your business. This is a decent neighbourhood."

"This motor belongs to Captain Cathcart," said Rose in cut-glass tones. "I am Lady Rose Summer and we are waiting for him. *You* go about your business, Constable."

"Not my fault," grumbled the policeman. "The porter in there, he phones and says there's a couple of prostitutes outside."

"Just go away," Rose was saying furiously when Harry and Becket joined them.

"This officer has accused us of being prostitutes," said Rose.

Harry turned hard black eyes on the constable. "I'm right sorry, sir," he said. "But it was that porter what told me."

"Just go about your duties," said Harry. The policeman touched his helmet and walked off.

"Now," said Harry, "what are you doing here?"

"Looking for Mr. Jones. We tried to talk to him at his shop but he escaped by the back way."

"Well, I tried as well, but he had warned the porter not to admit anyone. Let's get out of here. We need to talk. You are putting yourself at risk."

They went to the tea room opposite the haberdashery. Rose told Harry all they had found out. She said finally, "Are you sure that Jeffrey Biles was not our murderer?"

"I am not sure at all. He did not receive any visitors."

"Not even a lawyer?"

"He did not ask for one. But a lawyer would have been appointed to him before his trial."

"Then it must have been one of the guards at the prison," said Daisy.

Becket gave his wife an indulgent smile. "What on earth would a guard have to gain by killing him?"

"Money," said Daisy. "Maybe someone paid him to shut Jeffrey up."

"That sounds ridiculous," said Becket.

"Wait a minute," said Harry. "I will go to Kerridge tomorrow and ask if I can interview the guard. We must try everything. Perhaps Jones became so obsessed with Dolores and was furious when he found out she had become a tart that something in him snapped. I mean, why does he refuse to see us? Why did he leave by the back door of his shop rather than be confronted by Rose and Daisy?"

"I would like to come with you," said Rose.

"Don't you think it will be difficult to escape?" asked Harry. "Your parents must be wondering where you are."

"I told them I was going down to the East End to do charity work."

"Nonetheless, there is no need for all of us to turn up at the prison. It would occasion too much comment and a prison is no place for a lady."

"Oh, I wish I were a man," complained Rose.

Harry smiled at her. "I am so glad you are not. Now, I had better take you home."

Outside the earl's town house, Harry helped Rose down from the car. He bent and kissed her hand.

"When all this is over," he said, "we will find a way to get married."

"We may have to elope," said Rose.

"I am sure I will find a way to persuade your parents. I know they have told me I am not to see you, so find out some social engagement you are going to and telephone my office and I will try to meet you there."

Rose felt that wings were bearing her into the house. I really do love him, she thought, and then her face fell as Brum informed her in severe tones that Lady Polly was asking for her.

Rose went to her rooms first to change the drab clothes she had chosen to wear while detecting. She rang for Hunter and was dressed in a tea gown.

"There you are!" exclaimed Lady Polly. "Brum tells me that you arrived home in Captain Cathcart's car. We told you to have nothing to do with that man."

"He happened to be in the East End at the same time," said Rose, "and I was glad of an escort home."

"Did you go on your own?"

"No, Mrs. Becket accompanied me."

"That was not enough. Two of the footmen should have been with you. Now I want you to look your best tomorrow night. We are going to Mrs. Blenkinsop's musical evening and Lord Cherm's son, Roger, is going to be there. He has been travelling abroad, which is why he has not been seen at the Season before. He is eminently eligible."

The telephone was in Matthew's office. Rose stood on the first landing, watching the office door in the hall until she saw Matthew come out. He put on his hat and coat and left.

Rose darted down the stairs and telephoned Harry. "I'll look through my invitations," he said. "If I haven't got one to the Mrs. Blenkinsop's, I will manage to get invited somehow. Be careful. No more detecting."

The next day, Rose was informed that her father had gone to his club and that her mother was lying down with a headache, although Hunter, the lady's maid, confided that the "headache" was actually a cream treatment to whiten the skin and remove any tan and was supposed to take all day.

Rose decided to call on Daisy. Daisy greeted her with relief and delight. "I thought I was going to be stuck here all day. I told the captain I wanted to take up my duties as detective and he said I had to stay at home because of the baby. Men! What do you have in mind?"

"I want to see this Mr. Jones. I want to see what he looks like. I want to see if I can waylay him and speak to him."

"Do you think he's dangerous?"

"What can he do? With Harry trying to see him, he must know he is under suspicion and he won't make any rash moves."

"How did you get out?"

"Mama is enduring some treatment to bleach her tan and Father is at his club. We'll take the cab I've got waiting outside."

It took quite a long time to reach Notting Hill. Rain had begun to fall and the roads were a morass of mud and horse droppings. Carters, bus drivers, tram drivers, cab drivers and the few motor chauffeurs had no protection against the rain. They sat in the open, wearing oilskin hats and capes, with the rain pouring off them. Noise rose up around Rose and Daisy. A motor bus honked and banged, encouraged by shouts of "Whip behind, guv'nor!"

The buses were of all colours: red, blue, yellow, white, green, purple, orange and chocolate. Like the old stagecoaches, they all had names, such as The Favourite, The Atlas, the Royal Blue, The Royal Oak and The Wellington.

Hawkers still hawked their wares, but they seemed angry about their goods, whereas their grandfathers had been pleased. Instead of the old melodious chants, they bawled and yelled.

As they arrived at Notting Hill, the rain stopped and a watery sunlight gilded the muddy pavements. Rose paid the cabbie and they both stood, irresolute.

"We'll sit in the tea room," said Daisy. "Look, it's quite empty. We can get a table by the window and observe the haberdashery."

They ordered tea and biscuits and tried to watch the shop but the sun was making steam rise from the pavement and the window was steamed up. Rose kept rubbing a viewing circle with her handkerchief.

"Are you watching that shop?" asked the waitress.

Rose swung round. "No, I like to look at the people passing by."

"Cos Mrs. Jones over there wondered what you was up to."

With a bob of her head, the waitress indicated a woman sitting in the far corner.

"I shall go and put her mind at rest," said Rose. "Come, Daisy."

They approached the haberdasher's wife. Rose

judged her to be in her late twenties. She was wearing a long grey coat unseasonably trimmed with fur. A large grey hat was perched on top of her piled-up blonde hair. Her eyes were small and looked at them warily.

"I am Lady Rose Summer," said Rose. She quickly noticed her name meant nothing to Mrs. Jones. "We are sorry we upset you. My companion, Miss Levine. May we join you? We do not know this area."

"Please," said Mrs. Jones, looking flustered and delighted at the same time. She would tell her friends that an aristocratic and beautiful young lady had joined her for tea.

Rose signalled to the waitress to bring their tea things over. She smiled charmingly at Mrs. Jones. "Have you lived in Notting Hill for long?"

"Only for a few years," she said shyly. She spoke in a sort of strangled voice as if she was trying to kill any trace of a Cockney accent.

"The waitress said your husband is the haberdasher."

"Yes. I thought you were watching the shop."

Rose smiled. "Now why should that bother you?"

"It's my husband. He's ever such a suspicious man. It's all come on him lately. He jumps at shadows."

"Perhaps too much work?" suggested Rose.

"It shouldn't be. He's got plenty of staff."

"I was supposed to meet my fiancé for lunch," sighed Rose. "But he is always so busy. He is a private detective. My parents think that is a terribly common thing to be. He does have some fascinating cases, however. He is looking into the death of Dolores Duval."

"I read about that in the newspapers," said Mrs. Jones. "But they've got someone for it."

"Yes, her brother, Jeffrey Biles. But he hanged himself. Dolores was originally Betty Biles from Whitechapel."

Mrs. Jones suddenly bent her head. Rose realized with a jolt of shock that she was crying.

"My dear Mrs. Jones. I do not want to upset you."

She took out a handkerchief and blew her nose. Then she raised her head. "It's my husband, Mr. Jones. He used to talk about her the whole time. Then when he found out she'd become no better than she should be, he got bitter about it."

"He did not have any contact with Jeffrey Biles, did he?" asked Rose.

Mrs. Jones jumped to her feet, knocking her teacup over. She ran for the door.

The waitress had been watching them avidly and she now hurried over to clean the spilled tea from the table.

"Now what do we do?" asked Daisy.

"The steam has cleared from the windows. We'll watch the shop again. I want to see what kind of man he is."

They moved back to their original seat.

Rose looked at her fob watch. "It is nearly lunchtime. Look, that must be our Mr. Jones."

A tall thin man had emerged from the shop. He was holding Mrs. Jones tightly by the arm. She was crying as he hustled her off down the street.

"As she had read about the case in the newspapers, it's a wonder she did not recognize my name," said Rose. "What did you make of him?"

"He's a lot older than his wife," said Daisy. "But he's got a sort of weak face. I can't imagine him murdering anyone."

"I wonder how Harry is getting on," said Rose, "because I can't really think of what we can do here now."

Armed with a letter from Kerridge, Harry went to Pentonville Prison to interview the guard who had been on duty at the estimated time of Jeffrey's suicide.

He was told that the guard, Joseph Carver, had not come in for work. Harry saw the governor and got Carver's address.

"Whitechapel," he said to Becket when he came out of the prison. "All roads lead to Whitechapel. Our guard did not show up for work. His address is 5, Gerald Street."

London had been for a long time the home of the persecuted and exiled. Whitechapel was largely the refuge of European Jews. They brought a bustling energy and life to the area, but there were still pockets where the English residents stayed in filth and dirt, ground down by lives of poverty. Gerald Street was a narrow cavern flanked on both sides by dingy tenements.

"The smell is awful," said Harry. "Why don't they wash?"

"In what?" asked Becket. "They haven't any baths and the public baths cost money."

Becket stayed to guard the car while Harry mounted the stairs of number 5. Names were scrawled in plaster at the side of the doors. Halfway up the stairs, he made out the name "Carver."

He knocked on the door. Nearby a baby wailed, a caged linnet sang, and a man shouted something unintelligible. Harry knocked again. No reply.

He turned away. Then he turned back and tried the

door handle. The door was not locked. He moved cautiously inside, calling, "Mr. Carver?"

A blanket was hanging over the window, leaving the room in darkness.

Harry edged towards the window and pulled the blanket down. He turned round and surveyed the room. It had very little furniture. There was an armchair in front of the fireplace. Harry realized with a shock that he could see the top of a man's head.

Must have fallen asleep, he thought. He walked round the front of the armchair and stared down in horror. Carver—and surely it must be Carver—had had his throat slit. His clothes were matted with blood.

Harry went quickly to the window which overlooked the street and threw it up. He called down to Becket, "Get the police here as fast as you can."

Harry was wearing gloves and so he decided to do a search of the room. There was little to search. He found a box of photographs—Carver with other prison guards on some sort of outing and a birth certificate.

The bed was in a recess. Harry slid his hands under the mattress and pulled out a wad of five-pound notes.

The police arrived first, followed later by Kerridge himself. "I would like to get out of here," said Harry. "Can I make my statement at the Yard? I've already told the police I found a wad of fivers under the mattress."

"Did you find a weapon? Looks like it's been done by a razor."

"No, but he may have thrown it away outside— down a drain in the street."

"We'll get to it."

"I'll go downstairs and wait in the motor." Harry ran down the stairs and gulped down fresh air outside before climbing into the car beside Becket.

He told Becket what had happened. "I hope my Daisy is behaving herself," said Becket, looking worried. "We thought it was all over and finished, but it's beginning to look as if the murderer is still out there."

"He may have bribed the guard. That would explain the money under the mattress."

They waited a long time. Finally Kerridge emerged. "I think we'll pull in this Mr. Jones for questioning. He may have nothing at all to do with us, but I'd like to see what he's like."

"I'll meet you at Scotland Yard," said Harry. "I would like to see him for myself."

"Can't do that," said Kerridge. "I'll get a rocket for letting an amateur into a police interrogation. I'll telephone you and let you know how I get on. If you want to get away, you can call at the Yard tomorrow and we'll take your statement there."

Mrs. Blenkinsop, a society widow, had recently moved to a splendid house in Park Lane.

Lady Polly's face was plastered with white makeup. The de-tanning cream had only removed the brown in patches. "Who would have thought a Cairo tanning would last so long?" she mourned. "That is the trouble with middle-aged skin. Now I want you to be particularly charming to young Roger. A great catch."

Rose hoped Harry would be there. Then her heart sank as she remembered all the evenings in the past when they were officially engaged and he had failed to turn up. Her finger hurt. Her mother had ordered a jeweller to come round to the house and take the offending engagement ring off. It now resided in the depths of Rose's jewel box.

She missed Daisy's cheerful company. Rose was wearing a white chiffon gown with long lace sleeves and a lace panel at the front. On her head she wore a tiara of pearls. As she climbed down from the carriage, her taffeta and silk petticoats rustled. That rustle, thought Rose bitterly, was supposed to be seductive, but what was the point of appearing seductive if the very man one hoped to charm was not likely to attend?

When they were seated in the music room, Lady Polly nudged her daughter. "That's Roger there," she hissed, pointing with her fan.

Rose surveyed Roger. He was undoubtedly very handsome. He had thick wavy fair hair and a strong nose and firm mouth.

As if conscious of her gaze, he turned his head and gave her a half smile. Rose ducked her head and twiddled with the sticks of her ivory fan. "He smiled at you!" exclaimed Lady Polly. "You must flirt, girl."

Fortunately for Rose, any further lecture was cut short by the start of the concert. A heavily built German gentleman sang lieder, followed by a soprano who sang "I Dreamt That I Dwelt in Marble Halls." She received noisy and rapturous applause from an audience who did not have to dream about living in marble halls because they already did. The soprano was followed by a Pole who played Chopin with great verve and then came the interval.

Lady Polly stood up and called, "Elizabeth!" She pinched Rose's elbow. "Roger's mother. Be charming."

"Polly, my dear." Lady Cherm, who joined them, was unfashionably thin, to the point of emaciation. Her low-cut gown showed sharp bones.

"Where is your gorgeous boy?" cooed Lady Polly.

"Right there. Roger! Come and be introduced."

Roger came to join them. His eyes were grey and fringed with fair lashes. After the introductions were effected, Roger held out his arm to Rose. "Shall we walk a little before the next half? I find rout chairs demned uncomfortable."

Rose took his arm. "I have read a lot about you, Lady Rose," said Roger. "You do seem to have a lot of adventures."

"I hope they are over now," said Rose, looking around for Harry and not finding him. "I have not seen you at the Season before."

"I've been travelling. I adore seeing other countries." He began to describe his travels and Rose found herself becoming very interested. "I'll need to settle down one day," said Roger, fixing her with his clear grey gaze, "but it would need to be with someone as adventurous as myself."

Rose felt a pulse of attraction for him. Harry was such a difficult man. What would it be like to be free to travel the world with an adventurous husband?

"It's starting again," said Roger with a groan. "Not my thing. I say, would you like to go driving in the Park with me tomorrow?"

Rose was about to refuse, but then a spurt of rebellion prompted her to say, "I should like that very much."

Why should she forgo the chance of a drive with a handsome man for someone like Harry who, as usual, had not even bothered to show up?

Harry had been refused an invitation. Mrs. Blenkinsop had recently tried to hire him to find her lost dog and Harry had declined. She had not forgiven him. He wondered how he was going to be able to see Rose. He also realized that he could not afford to keep turning down minor cases and so he told his secretary to advertise in the newspapers for detectives. Daisy was not in a condition to go out detecting and he needed Becket with him as an assistant as well as a driver.

He was disappointed that Rose had not called him to tell him of any social engagements where he might meet her. He wrongly assumed that she would understand that he had been unable to secure an invitation.

Then he suddenly thought that at least Daisy could call on her and tell her all about the latest developments. Unfortunately, he forgot to tell Daisy why he had failed to appear the night before.

Rose listened in growing horror as Daisy told her of the death of the prison guard. She almost thought of cancelling her outing with Roger but then realized if she did so, her mother would be furious with her.

"I wonder how Kerridge got on with interviewing Jones," she said. "I would have loved to be there."

"What I was wondering," said Daisy, "was how a haberdasher from a shop in the Mile End Road could suddenly afford a large shop in Notting Hill, not to mention a flat in Chepstow Mansions."

"Do you mean he might have been some sort of criminal using the shop as a cover?"

"Something like that. I'm thinking of going back down the East End to make some inquiries. Can you come?"

Rose looked at the clock. Three in the afternoon. She planned long preparations to dazzle Roger. "I cannot, Daisy. I am going out driving with a gentleman and want to look my best."

"And who is this gentleman?"

"Lord Cherm's son, Roger. He is well travelled and is very interesting."

"And what about the captain?"

"Daisy, he promised to be at the Mrs. Blenkinsop's last night and he did not bother to come. Delighted as I am to see you, I feel he should have made a push to see me himself."

"Perhaps he was unable to get an invitation."

"Pooh, I happen to know he has done work for Mrs. Blenkinsop in the past. He does not care enough. If he had really loved me, he would not have become enamoured with Dolores."

Rose, much as she liked to consider herself democratic, felt that there was something seriously wrong when Harry could be charmed by a vulgar creature from the East End.

"I'll go myself," said Daisy.

Harry went to Scotland Yard. "How did you get on with Jones?" he asked Kerridge.

"Jones got a lawyer here very quickly. He acted the outraged shopkeeper. As we had nothing so far to connect him with either Carver or Biles, we had to let him go."

"What did you make of him?"

"I'm puzzled. He does seem a respectable man, rather weak and fussy. It would take a great stretch of my imagination."

"If he is innocent, why did he refuse to see me?"

"Perhaps he has something murky to hide other than murder."

"I wonder. He does seem to live in style and have a large shop. Quite a social jump-up from the East End. I think I'll go down there with Becket and ask around where the shop used to be."

D aisy had had the same idea. The shop was now an ironmonger's. She pushed open the door and went in.

A huge man in a brown overall stood behind the counter. Without Rose's purse to back her up, Daisy did not want to spend the small amount of money she had with her by buying items of ironmongery. She decided to be direct.

"I am working for the Cathcart Detective Agency," she said. "Did you know the previous owner, Mr. Jones?"

"I bought the shop from him, that's all," he said.

"The thing that puzzles me," said Daisy, "is how he got enough money out of the sale to buy that big shop up west?"

"Why don't you ask him?"

"I tried. Anyway, the police are questioning him today."

"I don't like nosy parkers." He came round the counter and loomed over her. "Do you know what happens to nosy parkers round here?"

Daisy turned to go.

"They end up in the river," he shouted.

Daisy reached for the door handle but a vicious blow struck her on the back of the head.

"I'll deal with you later," growled the shopkeeper.

He decided to close up. When Becket and Harry arrived, he was putting up the shutters.

Harry approached him. "I would like a word with you."

"Haven't got the time," he said. "Closing up."

"Bit early for that, isn't it?" asked Harry.

Becket got down from the car and stood beside Harry. Then Becket heard a faint cry from the shop. "Help me!"

The shopkeeper snarled, "Go away," and tried to get into the shop. Harry struck him a savage blow behind his legs with his stick and the man fell to the ground.

"See who's there, Becket," said Harry.

Becket ran into the shop. Then Harry, standing over the fallen shopkeeper, heard Becket howl, "It's Daisy. She's hurt bad."

The shopkeeper tried to struggle to his feet. Harry struck him over the head and he fell down again.

He went into the shop. "I'll tie that villain up. Help me with a shutter. We'll lift Daisy out and put her in the car and then get her to hospital. Take her to Saint Bartholomew's."

Harry found some rope behind the counter. He went out and tied the man up and dragged him by his heels into the shop. Then he brought a shutter and they gently lifted Daisy onto it. Daisy was moaning faintly, and as they lifted her, Harry saw with horror that the back of her gown was stained with blood.

Once Daisy had been lifted into the car and driven

off, Harry returned to the shop. He saw there was a telephone on the wall. Odd that a poor neighbourhood shop should boast a telephone, he thought, but he dialled Scotland Yard and told Kerridge about the events.

Then he phoned the earl's secretary and left a message for Rose that Daisy had been attacked and was now in hospital.

ELEVEN

I could lie down like a tired child,
And weep away the life of care
Which I have borne and yet must bear,
Till death like sleep might steal on me.

—PERCY BYSSHE SHELLEY

Rose was not at home for Harry's telephone call. She was out being driven in the Park by the handsome Roger. She found him more and more intriguing and felt she could listen to his stories for hours. His tales took her imagination flying to coral islands, to the minarets of Istanbul and the bustling excitement of New York.

He made her feel feminine, light and free. There was none of that aching, dark, brooding, frightening passion she often felt for Harry.

The earl had demanded to know who had rung and Matthew had told him about Daisy's predicament. The earl told his wife.

"Where is she?" demanded Lady Polly.

"Bart's."

"Then we must go immediately."

"I'll order the carriage," said the earl.

Daisy had been employed by them and the earl and

countess were diligent at looking after their staff. That Daisy was no longer in their employ did not matter. It was still their responsibility to take care of her.

They were escorted by a matron to outside a ward where Becket was sitting with his head in his hands.

"How is she?" demanded Lady Polly.

"I'm waiting to find out, my lady," said Becket, getting to his feet.

"We will have her removed to a private room as soon as possible," said the earl.

They waited in silence. Becket was too upset, too shy of them at the same time, to make any attempt at conversation.

At last a doctor approached them. "Mr. Becket," he said, "your wife is going to be all right, but I'm afraid Mrs. Becket has lost her baby."

"We are the Earl and Countess of Hadshire," said Lady Polly grandly. "We feel Mrs. Becket should be moved to a private room."

"We will do that as soon as she comes out of the operating theatre."

"May I see her?" pleaded Becket.

"It won't be long now. My lord, my lady, we have a more comfortable room for you to wait in. Follow me."

They had been waiting for half an hour when Rose arrived. "What on earth has happened to Daisy?" she asked.

Becket told her about the visit to the shop and then said in a stifled voice, "Daisy has lost the baby."

"How dreadful. How is she?"

"I don't know. They say they will let me see her soon."

"Where is Captain Cathcart?"

"He was guarding the villain when I left. When I get my Daisy out of here, I never want her to do any detecting again."

"And that goes for you, too, Rose," said Lady Polly angrily.

A doctor came in, a different one, and said, "Mr. Becket, you can have a few words with your wife now. She has had a bad concussion and lost a lot of blood."

They all got to their feet. "I think perhaps Mr. Becket should see her alone," he said.

Becket went off. Then Matthew Jarvis arrived. "I came, my lord, to see if I could be of any help."

"Good man. Go and see whoever you have to and get the billing for a private room for Mrs. Becket. She has lost her baby. Find out the best consultants in Harley Street for her and tell them to examine her as soon as possible. Make arrangements for proper food and strengthening wine to be delivered to her room."

"Very good, my lord."

The doctor came back. "I think you can spend a few minutes with Mrs. Becket. Follow me."

Daisy looked a small forlorn figure lying in the hospital bed. Her head was bandaged. Tears ran down Rose's face. She sat down by the bedside and took Daisy's hand.

Becket was on the other side of the bed, his face white with misery. "Do you know what they are saying, Rose?" whispered Daisy. "They say I may have lost the baby anyway. It was not a strong pregnancy."

"Shhh, dear. You must get strong and well again."

"Country air is what you need once you are out of here," said Lady Polly bracingly. "We will make arrangements to have you removed to Stacey Court, you and your husband, that is."

"You are very kind, my lady."

The doctor and a nurse reappeared. "I think Mrs. Becket should be left to rest," said the doctor.

"Find a room here for her husband," ordered the earl. "My secretary is around somewhere. Make the arrangements with him."

Back home, Rose thanked her parents for their care of Daisy. "I thought I never liked the gel," said Lady Polly with a sigh. "Then I remembered how she had saved your life and how brave she had been. It was the least we could do." And before Rose could thank them again, Lady Polly said briskly, "Now, to more important matters. How did you get on with Roger?"

"Very well."

"And when are you seeing him again?"

"We are to take luncheon together tomorrow, but now, in view of Daisy's predicament . . ."

"Piffle. She will be well looked after."

Rose went up to her room, wondering what to do about Roger. Roger seemed to her to present a golden world of travel and respectability, far away from getting attacked in the East End. Her parents would be so pleased. She would never have to worry again about Harry's fancy being taken by another woman, never again feel that burning misery she had experienced when he had promised to escort her to a ball or party and had failed to turn up.

Marriage to Roger would mean travel and companionship. Marriage to Harry, on the other hand, held only the promise of hurt and danger.

Harry stretched his bad leg out in front of him as he sat in a chair opposite Kerridge. "So do you think we have our murderer?"

"I'm sure we have, although Jones is swearing blind he's innocent of that."

It had transpired that Jones had not sold the shop in the Mile End Road, but had turned it over to Daisy's assailant, Pat Docherty. The shop had been used as a front. The police had wondered for quite a time where robberies from the ships at London's docks had gone to. Now, they knew. The cellars below the shop had been crammed with stolen goods. Jones had worked as the fence. Docherty had caved in after his arrest and told them everything, including the names of all the other men who had worked for Jones.

"As Jones knew so many villains, it stands to reason that although he may not have done the murders himself, he could easily have got one of his ruffians to do them for him."

"We're fingerprinting the lot of them, although the gun that shot Dolores had Lady Rose's fingerprints on it. Isn't society amazing? If Lady Rose had been Miss Bloggs of Nowhere, she'd be ready for a hanging about now."

"Don't even think about it. I'm off to the hospital to see Daisy."

Harry was told that Mrs. Becket was asleep and was conducted to the room given to Becket.

"How is she?" asked Harry.

"She's lost the baby. She has a bad concussion and lost a lot of blood but they say she is going to be all right."

"Docherty should be charged with murder. I thought he only hit her on the head."

"They say she would probably have lost the baby anyway. It was a weak pregnancy."

"I want you to stay here until she's better. I'll go home and pack up your clothes and shaving kit. And tell them to bill me for any expenses."

"Lord and Lady Hadshire have taken care of everything."

"Really? You amaze me. I'll be back shortly with your things."

Harry collected his car from where Becket had left it outside the hospital. He considered his changed circumstances as he drove back to Chelsea. Before he had started the agency, when he had little money, he had been content with Becket as his only servant. Then there was Phil, but Phil had left. He would hire two detectives to help him, and in the morning he would get his secretary to call an agency and employ a housekeeper and gentleman's gentleman. He would find an apartment for Daisy and Becket. Becket could work as his chauffeur and Daisy could be a lady of leisure.

During the next week, he longed to see Rose, but instructing his two new detectives and breaking in new staff left him little time to visit the hospital, and on each occasion he found Rose had just left.

Kerridge phoned him one day to say that they could not charge either Jones or Docherty with the murder of

Dolores because there was no proof. "But if they didn't do it, I'm sure they organized it," he said, "so Lady Rose does not have to worry about any of them any more."

Harry entered his office in the morning to be told that Lady Glensheil was waiting for him. He had worked for Lady Glensheil before.

Lady Glensheil was an imposing woman with a face like a Roman emperor.

"How can I help you?" he asked, ushering her into the inner office.

She sat down with a sigh. Her hat was decorated with a stuffed ptarmigan with little rubies for eyes. He wondered how she could bear the weight of it.

"I employ a lady's maid. Her name is Henrietta Thomson."

Harry had begun to take notes. He looked up sharply. "She did not once work for Dolores Duval, did she?"

"Not that I know of."

"Who was her last employer?"

"Lady Burridge. Thomson has excellent references."

"I think I know the woman. But first tell me your problem."

"Some of my jewellery has gone missing. I do not want to call in the police because most of the staff have been with me for a long time. I am having one of my tea afternoons. If you could come at five as a guest but observe the servants and this Thomson woman and tell me what you think . . ."

"Perhaps it would be better if you could sketch me a plan of the house, pointing out where her room is. When your guests arrive, keep her occupied and I will search her room."

"Thank you. I knew I could depend on you. Lady Rose and Lady Polly will be there."

The same morning, Rose visited Daisy. "Where's your husband?" she asked.

"Becket's gone out to buy me some fruit."

"Do you always call him Becket? What is his first name?"

"Reginald. I'm worried, Rose."

"The doctors say you will soon be restored to complete health."

"It's not that. Becket has found an apartment for us in Bloomsbury. He says it is very fine, three bedrooms. But I am to be the lady of the house. I am not to do any outside work at all. Rose, I will die of boredom."

"I am sure he can be persuaded to let you do something."

"I don't think so. He's become all masterful. You will do this, Daisy, and you will do that. I'm afraid I don't love him any more." A tear slid down Daisy's cheek.

Rose took her hand. "You are still suffering from shock. Once you get on your feet again, you will see things differently."

But when she left the hospital, Daisy's words rang like a dirge in her ears. "I'm afraid I don't love him any more." For Rose was seriously beginning to wonder if she loved Harry. She found herself thinking more and more about Roger. He was as fair as Harry was dark. He had none of Harry's brooding good looks. He was sunny and uncomplicated and he made it plain he thought she was wonderful.

Rose knew that unless *her* intentions were honourable, then she should not continue to see him.

• • •

When she arrived with her mother at Lady Glensheil's that afternoon, it was to find Harry was there. Her heart gave a lurch. Then, without even looking at her, he put down his teacup, muttered an excuse and left the room.

Rose's face flamed with humiliation. She could see some of the debutantes glancing at her in a sly way and then whispering to one another behind their fans.

And then a welcome voice in her ear said, "What a delight to see you again so soon."

Roger stood smiling down at her. "You did not mention at luncheon that you would be here."

"Mama handles my social engagements. I did not even know until this afternoon that I was invited."

Roger fetched a chair and sat down next to her. Now the debutantes were scowling and Rose experienced a little stab of triumph.

Harry found the lady's maid's room by studying the sketch of the house that Lady Glensheil had given him. Most of the servants were on duty at the tea party or in the kitchens, and so the upper part of the house was quiet. He tried the door. It was locked. Thankful that he had brought his lock picks with him, he got to work.

At last he got the door open and went inside. He began to search diligently, opening drawers, searching in the wardrobe and under the mattress. He could not find any jewels. The lady's maid had a jewel box but it only contained a few trinkets.

He lifted the rug and checked the floorboards but they looked as if they had lain undisturbed for years.

He sat down in an upright chair by the window and looked carefully around.

Downstairs, Lady Glensheil said sharply, "Where are you going?"

"I am going to my room to collect something, my lady."

"You will stay where you are until I give you permission to leave."

Upstairs, still in the lady's maid's room, Harry noticed a small strand of thread by the window. He got up and lifted one of the thick lined curtains, weighing it in his hand. He then went to the worktable and took out a pair of scissors. He deftly unpicked the deep hem of one curtain and shook it. An emerald necklace dropped to the floor, followed by a diamond brooch. He rapidly unpicked the hem of the other curtain and found a cameo brooch, an amethyst ring and a pearl bracelet.

He went rapidly downstairs to the hall and phoned Scotland Yard and left a message for Kerridge. Then he went to join Lady Glensheil. "You were right," he whispered. "Get a couple of your men to lock her up until the police arrive."

Lady Glensheil signalled to a hovering footman. "I want two of you to take Thomson here and lock her up until the police arrive. Not in her room. The library will do."

Thomson jumped to her feet. "Why are you doing this to me?"

"You are a thief," Lady Glensheil said coldly. "Take her away."

The guests sat as if turned to stone, some of them with teacups halfway to their lips as a screaming and protesting Thomson was dragged away.

"Just domestic trouble," said Lady Glensheil. "Do not let it spoil my party." Rose looked across at Harry but he was talking intently to Lady Glensheil and did not seem aware of her existence.

She leaned across and said to her mother, "I have a headache. I would like to leave."

Lady Polly smiled indulgently at Roger. "Would you mind escorting my daughter home?"

"I would consider it an honour."

It was then that Harry saw Rose. He hurried round the tables to catch up with her. Lady Polly watched him with furious eyes and just as he was passing her she thrust out her parasol and tripped him up.

Harry fell across the table, sending cups and glasses flying. He straightened himself up painfully because his bad leg was hurting. His suit was covered in jelly and cake. He hobbled quickly out of the room to catch up with Rose.

He was just in time to see her driving off with Roger. "Rose!" he shouted, but his voice was drowned out by the sound of Roger's car's engine.

Thomson paced up and down the library, looking for escape. The library was on the ground floor and so the windows were barred.

She stopped her pacing and looked at the fireplace. She walked over and removed the screen and bent down. It was an old, wide chimney with climbing rungs for the chimney sweep's boys.

She took off her hat and threw it on the floor.

Bending her head, she went into the fireplace and began to climb. When she reached to top, she let out a strangled sob because her way was blocked by the chimney pot. Standing on the last rung, she stretched her arms up and pushed sideways with manic strength. The pot gave a little. She pushed harder until it gave and fell onto the roof and began to roll down to the edge.

Kerridge had just arrived with police officers when they heard a rumbling sound and a crash.

One of the policemen ran outside and then came running back. "It's a chimney pot, sir, fallen off the roof."

"The library chimney," said Harry, who had just joined them wearing one of Lord Glensheil's suits. "She might have escaped that way."

They unlocked the library door. The maid's hat lay in front of the fireplace and a final cascade of loose soot came falling down the chimney.

Thomson knew that the house next door was empty, the owners having gone to the country. She smashed the lock on a back door with a rock and let herself in. Far above her, she could hear the police searching the roofs.

She stripped naked in the kitchen and scrubbed herself clean at the sink. Then, still naked, she ran upstairs and into a lady's bedroom. Quickly, she put on underclothes, gown and hat. She found a reticule and transferred the contents of her own sooty one into it.

She ran from room to room, ransacking the drawers and picking up as many portable valuables as she could. With a sigh of relief, she found a bag of guineas carelessly left in the bedside table in the master bedroom. She also found a spare set of keys, which by their size she guessed were for the front door.

Thomson walked down to the front door. She picked a parasol out of the stand by the door and took a deep breath. Unfurling it to hide her face, she unlocked the front door, locked it behind her, and strolled down the street. She hailed a cab at the corner.

"Where to?" asked the cabbie.

"I'll let you know. Just drive on."

Kerridge and Harry went to St. Stephen's Tavern that evening to worry over this new development.

"It's a pity Lady Glensheil did not remember that the neighbours were away from home until hours later," said Kerridge. "A sooty woman running around London would have been easy to find, but there were all the signs that she had washed herself and stolen clothes."

"Do you think it is possible she is a murderess?" asked Harry. "Might Jones be telling the truth?"

"It's hard to believe. We never even thought of her. What we should have considered was the oddity of a seemingly respectable lady's maid taking a post with a well-known tart. It's a class thing and I fell for it. Me! If she had been some slattern from the East End, I would have been suspicious."

"If she is a murderess, is Lady Rose is any danger?"

"I shouldn't think so. Why?"

"I think that perhaps Thomson went to considerable lengths to persuade Jeffrey to make her look guilty.

She must be deranged and she may have a personal vendetta against her."

Harry looked uneasy. "I am barred from her home. I've hired two detectives. One of them, Bernie King, is very young and sharp. I think I'll put him on to following her discreetly."

Rose's mind was in a turmoil over the rival attractions of Roger and Harry. She decided the next morning to slip out of the house, go to Harry's office and ask him outright if he loved her and if they were getting married and what the scene at Lady Glensheil's had all been about.

She escaped from the house when Brum wasn't looking, knowing the butler would immediately inform her parents.

She hailed a cab and gave the driver instructions as to how to get to Harry's office in Buckingham Palace Road.

Her heart was beating hard. It was only when she descended the carriage that a wave of helplessness engulfed her. Harry would say that of course he wanted to marry her and then he would go on behaving as usual. And he had not even troubled to tell her what all that fuss at the tea party had been about.

Upstairs, Bernie King had just received a phone call from Harry, who was still at home, ordering him to follow Lady Rose. Bernie was a thin, black-haired man in his early thirties. He had been in the police force but had been attracted by Harry's advertisement. He grabbed his coat and glanced down from the window. He knew what Lady Rose looked like, Harry's secretary having provided him with a photograph from a society magazine.

To his surprise he saw her standing on the pavement outside. He ran lightly down the stairs. He was glad that Lady Rose did not know what he looked like.

She was climbing into a cab. Bernie hailed another cab and followed her. He saw her entering her home. He moved a little way around the square where he could observe the house without being obvious.

At noon, when he was beginning to feel thoroughly bored, he saw a smart motor car drive up and a handsome fair-haired man descended and went into the house. Bernie groaned. If the young man had come to take Lady Rose driving, how could he follow?

The square was deserted. He strolled past the car, looking to right and left. When he came abreast of the car, he leaped into the rumble—that rear seat for luggage—and finding a carriage rug, pulled it over himself. If he was discovered, he would need to rely on his boss to get him out of trouble.

After ten minutes, he felt the car dip and the man's voice say, "I thought we would take a spin down by the river."

Rose's voice answered, "What a lovely day!"

Bernie lay for what seemed to him a long time. The couple did not talk much because of the sound of the engine.

At last, the cab stopped. "I believe this is quite a good place for lunch," he heard the man say. "We can have lunch in the garden."

She answered something as their voices faded away.

After a few minutes, Bernie cautiously lifted his head. He recognized the Star and Garter at Richmond.

Some people were passing, so he ducked down again. Then he tried again. No one around.

He nipped out of the rumble and strolled into the pub. He went to the bar and ordered a half pint of beer and then carried it to a table where he could look out into the garden.

He felt a pang of envy. They looked such a handsome, carefree couple. He took out his notebook and began to write.

His stomach rumbled after half an hour but he did not want to order any food and then lose them if they suddenly decided to leave. He regretted his decision after an hour.

Just when he thought they meant to spend the whole afternoon in Richmond, he saw the man calling for the bill and Lady Rose adjusting her driving veil.

He left quickly, getting a sour look from the barkeep, who obviously did not favour customers who only ordered one drink and stayed for a long time.

Bernie went outside, looked around, and jumped back in the rumble.

As the couple approached the car, he heard the man say, "Are you going to the masked ball at the Twenders tonight?"

"I believe so."

He laughed. "I have a secret. I have already asked your parents' permission to escort you."

"How delightful," he heard Lady Rose say. "I must thank you for lunch."

"The pleasure is all mine, I assure you."

The car drove off. Bernie planned to escape when they stopped outside Lady Rose's home. He knew if he stayed in the rumble, he might end up locked in a garage somewhere.

He waited when he heard them descend, waited until he heard them mount the steps to the front door. He poked his head up. The man was kissing Lady Rose's hand. He quickly jumped down from the rumble, glad the enamoured couple had eyes only for each other.

When he was back in the office, he went in to see Harry and delivered his report. Bernie was not yet up to the mark in society gossip and did not know of Harry's on/off engagement to Rose. So he was taken aback by the blind fury on Harry's face when he delivered his report.

"Have I done something wrong?" asked Bernie plaintively.

Harry pulled himself together with an effort. "No, you have done very well."

"Would you like me to follow Lady Rose to this masked ball?"

"No, I shall be going myself. I would like you now to go to Bart's Hospital and visit Mrs. Becket and ask her if there is anything she or her husband needs."

When Bernie had gone, Harry telephoned Lady Glensheil. "That man who left your tea party with Lady Rose yesterday," he said. "Who is he?"

"Oh, that must be the catch of the Season, the Honourable Roger Sinclair, Lord Cherm's eldest son. Captain Cathcart, I am sending you a cheque for finding my jewels and exposing that dreadful woman."

After Harry had finished talking to her, he replaced

the receiver and sat staring bleakly into space. He had an awful feeling he was losing Rose.

Becket had gone to survey the new apartment. Daisy lay listlessly in her hospital bed. She was grateful to the earl and countess for having got her a private room, but at that moment she would have welcomed the company of a general ward.

The door opened and a nurse said, "Visitor for you."

Bernie entered the room. Daisy looked at this stranger. He was tall and thin with black hair and a sallow, clever face and a beaky nose and long humorous mouth.

"I'm Bernie King," he said, drawing a chair up to the bed. "I work for Captain Cathcart. He asked me to call on you and see if you need anything."

"I would like some books," said Daisy. "The ones Lady Rose has left for me are a bit too clever. I would like some romances."

"I'll get them to you. Now, how are you?"

"Pretty awful. I keep thinking about the baby."

"You'll have others."

Daisy shuddered. "Not if I can help it. Don't let's talk about me. Let's talk about the case. What's been happening?"

Bernie told her all about Thomson, the lady's maid. Then he told her how he had been asked to follow Lady Rose and keep an eye on her. He described the trip to Richmond and how he had hidden in the rumble.

Daisy began to look animated. She pulled herself up higher on her pillows. "Oh, Gawd," she said. "The poor captain. Rose does get tired of him not turning up to take her places."

"They're going to a fancy dress ball tonight. Don't worry. The captain's going as well."

"Wait a bit. Does he think this lady's maid might have done those murders?"

"Could be."

"But where would her brother have come into it?"

"This Thomson might have persuaded the brother somehow. Say, he called on Dolores for money and she got tired of him and threw him out. Thomson hears about the will leaving everything to him. She encourages him to call again. But this time he finds his sister dead. Stunned, he does what Thomson tells him, takes some jewellery. Thomson then tells him later that they can pin the murder on Lady Rose. She finds out about Madame De Peurey. They both go to Paris. Jeffrey is sent out to follow Rose. Madame de Peurey is killed and Thomson herself, maybe dressed as a man, maybe not, tries to push Lady Rose in the Seine and leaves that note."

"I wish I were out of here. I used to be Lady Rose's companion before I got married. I miss being with her. What about you? How did you come to be working for the captain?"

"I was in the police force. I was getting bored pounding the beat and saw the captain's advertisement. He liked me and got Mr. Kerridge to intercede so that I could quit the force immediately. They weren't bothered. I was only an ordinary copper."

"You're obviously a Londoner."

"That's me. Brought up in Whitechapel."

"Me too," said Daisy. "You'll never believe it, but I used to be a chorus girl at Butler's."

"Gosh, I used to go to Butler's."

They began to reminisce about places in Whitechapel and people they had known. Daisy was happy for the first time in a long time. Then the door opened and Becket came in.

Daisy introduced them. Becket glared at Bernie.

"Got to go," said Bernie. "I'll bring you those books."

"What books?" demanded Becket after Bernie had left.

"Never mind," said Daisy in a dull voice. "I want to go to sleep now."

TWELVE

Let us have a quiet hour,
Let us hob-and-nob with Death.

— ALFRED, LORD TENNYSON

Roger had found out from Lady Polly that Rose planned to go to the ball as a Roman lady and delighted her when he arrived to escort her attired as a Roman soldier.

She could not help noticing that he had very fine legs.

Rose knew she would be the envy of every debutante there and was human enough to look forward to it after having been regarded as one of society's failures.

She decided to forget all about Harry and enjoy the evening. Rose called on Aunt Elizabeth before she left, as that lady was leaving for Scotland on the following day.

"You look much happier than I have ever seen you," said Aunt Elizabeth. "Go off with your young man and have a splendid time."

Harry was furious. Always anxious to help those in need, he had employed a retired detective,

Tom Barnard, as his gentleman's gentleman. In pressing his evening coat, Tom had left a glazed iron mark on the back.

"What am I to do now?" raged Harry.

Tom was fat and round and his face never betrayed any emotion. His wife, Martha, who now worked as Harry's housekeeper, was built along the same lines and she had the same sort of impassive face.

"Why did you not leave the job to your wife?" he raged.

"I thought valeting was to be my duty, sir," said Tom.

The door opened and Martha came in carrying a black velvet evening cloak. She curtsied and said, "I found this in your wardrobe, sir. If you put it about your shoulders and wear your black mask, it will look very dashing and I will have your evening jacket restored tomorrow."

"Oh, very well," snapped Harry. Then he relented. "I know you are new to all this. I will get Becket to spend a day with you, Tom, and he will instruct you as to what to do. Now, help me on with my clothes!"

Roger swung Rose round in the steps of a waltz. He was feeling elated. He had received permission from Rose's parents to pay his addresses to her. Nestling in a little pouch attached to his belt was an engagement ring.

After the waltz had finished and the guests were beginning to move towards the supper room, he whispered, "Come out onto the terrace with me. I have a present for you."

Rose hesitated. But he had said nothing about a

proposal. "Very well," she said, "but just for a few moments. I am quite hungry. An unfashionable thing to say."

They walked to the long French windows at the end of the ballroom and he ushered her out onto the terrace.

To Rose's alarm, Roger got down on one knee and took her hand. "Rose," he said earnestly, gazing up into her eyes. "I—"

The terrace windows opened and a masked devil stepped out. Roger looked round in irritation. To Roger's horror, a gun appeared in the devil's hand and a female voice said, "Get up, you, and the pair of you walk down into the garden."

Roger got to his feet and stared in terror at the masked woman. "Is this a joke?"

"No joke. Move."

For a moment Roger stood paralysed with fear and then his bladder gave.

"Move," ordered the woman.

They walked down the steps into the darkness of the garden.

When they were deep in the darkness, the woman removed her mask. In the dim moonlight filtering through the trees, Rose recognized the maid who had been dragged out of the tea party.

"Why are you doing this?" she asked.

"Does it matter?" jeered Thomson. "Well, I'll tell you. You and that captain of yours have ruined all my plans. I kill you, he suffers. You flounce around London society without a care in the world. Now you know what it is like to be frightened."

"I've got nothing to do with this," gasped Roger. "This is between you and Rose."

"What a coward you are! What do you think of your precious beau now, Lady Rose? Cringing and pissing himself. Well, he's in the wrong place at the wrong time."

"Thomson," said Rose. "You were Dolores Duval's lady's maid. You murdered her."

"Why not? The trollop would have come to a bad end anyway."

Harry had been scouring the supper room for Rose. At last, a debutante said with a giggle, "If you are looking for Lady Rose, she went out on the terrace with Mr. Sinclair."

Harry ran to the French windows and let himself out. He stared around.

Then, from down in the garden, he heard a man's voice pleading, "Please let me go."

Harry seized his stick and moved silently and quickly down into the garden.

"It's no use begging," he heard a cold female voice say. "You're first."

Roger fell to his knees and burst into tears.

Rose gazed coldly at Thomson. If she had to die, then she would do so with dignity.

Thomson raised the gun. Then an arm brandishing a stick with a gold knob came out of the darkness and struck her a vicious blow on the head. Thomson collapsed on the ground.

Harry gathered Rose in his arms. "There now, my sweet," he said. "It's all over now."

"She confessed to the murder," said Rose. "I heard her. Roger heard her."

"You!" Harry barked at Roger. "Get up off the ground and go into the house and telephone the police."

"I can't," wailed Roger. "I . . . I've wet myself."

Harry looked at him in disgust. "Come, Rose. You will need to do it while I guard this creature. You, Mr. Sinclair, will need to wait for questioning. Here, take my cloak."

Rose hurried off into the house. She drew aside her hostess and told her the police were to be called immediately. There was a murderer in the garden. The alarmed hostess ordered footmen to go into the garden and then called the police.

"There is no need to alarm your guests," said Rose. "If you could find us a quiet room."

She was led to a study to await Harry.

Rose sank down into a chair and began to cry. She was crying not only over the fear of having nearly been killed but because the dream of Roger had been exploded.

When she heard footsteps approaching the study, she hurriedly dried her eyes. Roger came in wearing Harry's cloak. He slumped down in another chair and buried his head in his hands. Then Harry came in followed by footmen carrying the unconscious Thomson. Harry ordered them to lay her on the floor and then knelt down beside her.

He raised her head and looked at Rose. "She's still alive. I would not have liked the complications if I had killed her." He turned to one of the footmen. "Fetch brandy."

He pulled a chair up next to Rose and held her hand. "Why did you go out on the terrace?"

"Roger said he had a present for me. He said it would only take a few minutes."

"And what was the present?"

"I don't know. That awful Thomson creature appeared with a gun and ordered us down into the garden."

Harry surveyed Roger with contempt. "You may as well give it to her now."

"I must have lost it," mumbled Roger, wondering whether it might be possible to die of shame. During his many travel adventures, he had always been surrounded by a protective retinue of servants and had never before been in any danger at all. All he wanted to do now was to get as far away from Rose as possible.

"Here's the brandy. Pour Lady Rose a stiff measure," Harry ordered.

The door opened and Kerridge walked in with Inspector Judd and six policemen.

"That's her," said Harry. "Get her off to the prison hospital. I want her well enough to stand trial." Rose let out a little sigh of relief as the lady's maid was carried out.

"Now Lady Rose," said Kerridge, "we'll need to take a statement from you."

"Can't it wait until tomorrow?" asked Harry.

"It's all right," said Rose. "I'll do it now."

Roger trembled. She would tell them how he had pleaded for his own life. But Rose, in a flat little voice, merely described how they had both been forced to walk down into the garden and how Thomson had confessed to the murder.

Roger corroborated her statement and then pleaded to be allowed to go home. He left the room without saying goodnight to Rose or offering to return Harry's cloak.

Lady Polly was standing by the drawing room window. Her husband was sleeping in an armchair behind her. "What can be keeping her?" fretted Lady Polly. "It's nearly dawn."

A gentle snore was the only reply she got.

And then a car stopped outside. To her alarm, Lady Polly saw Harry helping Rose out.

"Wake up!" she screeched at her husband. "She's arrived! She's with that terrible Cathcart. Oh, what went wrong? Roger was supposed to propose to her."

Rose had not taken a house key with her. Lady Polly ran down the stairs as she heard the loud sound of the door knocker. She flung open the door and howled, "What is the meaning of this?"

"We will tell you all," said Rose. "Something terrible happened."

In the drawing room, where her father was now awake, Rose told them about the happenings of the evening.

"This is all your fault," said the earl, glaring at Harry.

"How can it be?" asked Rose. "He saved my life. Roger was no help. He would have run away if she had let him. All he did was wet himself."

"You must not say such things," exclaimed Lady Polly. "Captain Cathcart has led you into danger."

"It all started when I went to see Dolores and found her dead," said Rose. "If I had not been so stupid as to go and see her, then I would never have been involved or in danger. You must thank Captain Cathcart for saving my life and then let me go to bed. I am weary."

"I suppose thanks are in order," said the earl. "Go off with you, Rose. We'll talk more about this tomorrow."

"I must go to Scotland Yard tomorrow," said Rose, "and I would like Captain Cathcart to escort me."

"Oh, very well," said Lady Polly.

Rose left the room and Harry watched her go with sad eyes. Bernie had given him a very detailed report of that outing to Richmond. Harry guessed that Rose had enjoyed such easy company, such fashionable company, and thought she could please her parents by marrying such an unexceptional young man.

"I had better leave as well. I will call for your daughter just before noon. She is very tired."

When he had left, the earl grumbled, "I'm afraid we're stuck with him. But did you see his evening coat? Great shiny mark of the iron on the back of it. No gentleman should go out of the house like that."

Lady Polly said in a weary voice, "If he had been a gentleman like Roger, then our daughter might be dead. We'll need to let him marry her."

Harry appeared early in the office the next morning. After telling Bernie the events of the previous night, he said, "I've got a couple of small cases for you, but before that, I would like you to go to the hospital and make sure Mrs. Becket is all right. I have asked Mr. Becket to spend the day with my new servants and instruct them in their duties."

Bernie brightened. He seized his coat. "Mrs. Becket wanted some romances. I'll buy some from a bookshop on the way there."

Daisy smiled when Bernie entered her hospital room.

"I've got you the books you wanted," said Bernie. He read off the titles. "*The Duke's Passion, Lady Jane's Dilemma,* and *Shop Girl to Countess.*"

"Sounds just the thing. I should be out of here by tomorrow." Daisy's bandages had been removed. She put a hand up to the shaved part of her head and said, "I must look a fright."

"No, you look fine."

"Sit down, Mr. King."

"Bernie, please."

"Then sit down, Bernie. Has anything else happened?"

Bernie told her all about the drama in the garden and the arrest of Thomson. "Oh, that is wonderful," said Daisy when he had finished. "Rose will have nothing to worry about now. I do miss her. I liked being companion to Rose. We were like sisters."

"But you're married now and have a new home to go to."

A shadow crossed Daisy's expressive little face and she plucked nervously at the blankets.

"You must be mourning for your baby," said Bernie sympathetically.

"I feel unnatural because I'm not. You know how the upper classes say the lower classes don't have the same fine sensitive feelings as they have. Maybe it's true."

"Rubbish."

"I feel a failure as a wife, that's all. Now I'm to be a lady of leisure. What am I going to do with myself all day? I wish I could go back to being a companion to Rose. I wish . . ."

Daisy bit her lip in consternation. She had been on

the point of saying she wished she had never got married. Her eyes filled with tears.

"Here, now," said Bernie. "What can I do to cheer you up? I know, I'll start to read one of those books to you. You just lie back and listen."

He started to read, using different voices for the characters, until Daisy began to laugh. Then she said contritely, "I shouldn't be laughing."

"Course you should. Best medicine there is."

The door opened and Lady Polly came in, followed by a footman carrying a large basket of fruit.

She eyed Bernie. "Who is this person?"

"Not a person, my lady. Mr. King works for Captain Cathcart and he has brought me some books."

"I'll be off," said Bernie hurriedly. Daisy sadly watched him go.

"Now," said Lady Polly, "I have had my servants move all your belongings from Chelsea to your new home. My maids have cleaned your flat and everything is ready for you."

"Thank you, my lady."

"What is this trash you are reading?" asked Lady Polly, picking up *Lady Jane's Dilemma*.

"Just some romances. I didn't feel like reading anything heavy."

Lady Polly flicked the book open to the first page. "How is Lady Rose?" asked Daisy, but Lady Polly had become absorbed in the romance and did not hear her.

Rose sat silently beside Harry as he drove her to Scotland Yard. It was raining so she was wearing an oilskin coat, hat and goggles and shielding her head with a large umbrella. There was no danger of the umbrella being whipped away because the traffic was so bad, the motor seemed only able to inch along.

She remembered the sunny day with Roger at Richmond. It seemed very far away now.

At Scotland Yard, Rose took off her wet outer clothes with relief and followed Harry to Kerridge's office.

"Come in, Lady Rose," said Kerridge. "Are you recovered from your ordeal?"

"I hope so," said Rose. "I gather you want a detailed statement."

"My officer there will take it down. Just begin at the beginning."

Harry watched Rose anxiously as she began to speak. She described the events of the evening but without describing Roger's cowardice.

When she had finished, Kerridge said in a fatherly voice, "Thank you. I'll let the captain take you home now. You will need more rest."

"Actually, I think I will go and see Daisy."

"I'll take you there," said Harry quickly.

Rose gave him a small bleak smile. "I would rather see Daisy alone, if you don't mind."

"Then I shall drive you to the hospital. I suggest when you are ready to leave that you telephone Matthew Jarvis and get him to send a carriage for you."

Another silent journey while Harry tried to think of things to say while Rose sat beside him, her back ramrod-straight and her face shielded by the large umbrella.

At the hospital, Harry made to accompany her into

the building, but Rose said, as if speaking to a stranger, "No, leave me. I shall do very well."

And Harry sadly watched her go.

Daisy smiled as Rose walked in. "Your mother has just left. Lady Polly has been so kind."

Rose divested herself of her rain clothes and sat down wearily. "Tell me all about it," said Daisy.

"I am tired of talking about it," said Rose, but once more she described what had happened.

When she had finished, Daisy asked, "But did Roger, Mr. Sinclair, not try to rescue you?"

"It was awful, Daisy. When we first went out on the terrace and he got down on one knee, I knew he was going to propose. And I would have accepted! But then he became so frightened he begged Thomson to let him go. He was prepared to run away and leave me to my fate. I thought he was so strong and adventurous and yet he just crumbled."

"Not like the captain?"

"No, not like him."

"Your parents must be very grateful to the captain. Before she left, Lady Polly said, 'I'll need to let them marry now.'"

"I don't think I want to marry Harry."

"Go on!"

"You know, Daisy, I am tired of being society's rebel. When I was with Roger, things seemed so gay and easy. I began to see how happy I would be with someone cheery and undemanding. I do not want any more adventures. But don't look at me like that. You have your Becket, and all's well that ends well."

"I don't want to be married," said Daisy in a small voice. "I want to go back to the way things were."

"You are depressed because of the loss of your baby."

"I'm not. Not now. I feel unnatural. I feel the whole pregnancy was a dream and my marriage as well. I sometimes wake up and think I'm back in Belgrave Square with you. Then I realize I'm not and I cry."

"I'm sure we are both suffering from shock."

"Maybe. I had another visitor this morning. Bernie King. He works for the captain. He brought me some nice trashy books to read." Daisy giggled. "Lady Polly took one away with her."

"And what is this Bernie King like?"

"Ever so amusing. He comes from Whitechapel, same as me. Oh, Rose, what am I to do? I want a divorce."

Rose looked alarmed. "Daisy, once you are out of here and established, you will feel better. Besides, we are moving to the country soon and Mama has already said that you and Becket can come with us so that you may have some fresh air. So we will be together like the old times."

"Well, that's at least something," sighed Daisy. "But the old times will never come back now."

Harry and Kerridge had been told that Thomson was now conscious and they went to the prison hospital, where she was chained to the bed.

Her eyes glittered with fury as she looked at them. "How could you behave so wickedly?" asked Kerridge.

"What would you know about it?" she spat out. "You, the bourgeois and you, the slumming aristocrat, playing at being a detective. Do you know what it's like to be brought up in poverty? Then have to work one's way up through the ranks of servants to become a lady's maid? Always having to smile and crawl and watch people stuffing themselves with mountains of food while there are people starving in this country? Pah. Jeffrey was an easy tool. He kept calling for money and she would only give him a little at a time. He grew discontented. Then this Dolores said she did not want him coming around any more. She was getting threatening letters and she did not want anyone to know of her previous existence down the East End.

"Then Jeffrey told me that she had left a will leaving everything to him. I worked on him. I persuaded him that if I could get his sister out of the way, then he would inherit everything and he could pay me half for my trouble.

"He hummed and hawed until the last day, when he tried to talk to her and she screamed she never wanted to see him again. I gave him some of her jewels and told him to leave it to me.

"I thought Lady Rose would be accused and we would be free from suspicion, but of course I should have known an aristocrat is never under suspicion. It's one law for the rich and one for the poor."

"It's the same law for all," said Kerridge. "You will be hanged by the neck until you are dead, and good riddance."

When they left the hospital, Harry asked Kerridge, "Did Jones write those letters?"

"Yes, he's admitted to it."

"I haven't been pestered by the press," said Harry.

"We're keeping it quiet until the trial. Amazingly, none of the guests at the ball seems to have known what really went on. So what are your plans now?"

"More detective work," said Harry. "Lost dogs, scandals to be covered up, that sort of thing."

"What about Lady Rose?"

"I don't understand you."

"Are you getting married?"

"You'll be the first to know."

But Harry could not bear the idea of a rejection. He had a feeling that if Rose refused him, it would be final.

Rose longed for the departure for the country. Her brief popularity had gone. It was put about that she had turned the catch of the season down. The Duchess of Warnford told everybody who would listen that she had discovered in Paris that Rose was seriously unconventional and would probably remain a spinster until the end of her days.

Daisy, too, longed for the day of departure. She was borne to her new home in Bloomsbury. Becket then had to go off immediately to chauffeur Harry.

The flat faced north. It was furnished in the heavy, oppressive furniture of the last century. The windows were shrouded in blinds, net curtains and heavy damask curtains and the rooms were dark.

The flat consisted of a long corridor with the rooms leading off it. Daisy removed her hat and sat down in the parlour and stared bleakly around. She remembered how she had longed for a home of her own and wondered what had happened to her.

Harry had installed a telephone. Daisy eyed it. Then

she picked up the receiver and asked to be connected to Harry's office number. The secretary answered and Daisy, trying to disguise her voice, asked for Mr. Bernie King. "Who is calling, please?"

"His sister," said Daisy, hoping Bernie had one.

His cheery voice came on the phone. "Bernie, it's me, Daisy," she said. "I'm going mad with boredom. Is there any chance you could meet me for a cup of tea?"

She waited anxiously. "There's a Lyon's tea shop at Victoria, near the station. Know it?"

"Yes."

"I'll meet you there in an hour."

"Who was that?" asked Becket, who was sitting in a chair in the outer office.

"Just my sister," said Bernie.

I wonder what your husband would make of this," said Bernie, as he and Daisy sat over muffins and tea in Lyon's tea shop.

"I'm not doing anything wrong," said Daisy. She wondered if Bernie had noticed her hat, a straw cartwheel embellished with fat pink and yellow pansies. "My husband is working all day and I felt I had to get out."

"When do you leave for the country?"

"Next week."

"Are you looking forward to it?"

"I'm a city girl. Stacey Court is very quiet."

"How long will you be away?"

"Just a couple of weeks. It was Lady Polly's idea. She thinks fresh air would be good for me."

"Two weeks isn't a long time. It'll go quickly."

"May I see you from time to time when I get back?"

"I don't know, Daisy, I like you lots, but it doesn't seem right."

"I'm allowed friends," exclaimed Daisy.

"Of course, friends." Bernie gave Daisy's hand a little squeeze. "What else?"

D aisy prepared lamb chops for Becket's supper. She looked around the large high-ceilinged kitchen and reflected that soon she would at least be occupied in cleaning the flat. Her husband had said nothing about hiring help, and anyway, Daisy was sure they could not afford it.

When Becket came home, she served supper in their dining room. Becket looked about him with pride. "I say, Daisy, isn't this marvellous? Our new home at last."

"You know," said Daisy cautiously, "I am trained to type and take shorthand. It will be very dull for me, being here on my own all day. I could find a job and hire someone to clean."

"Nonsense. You're my wife and a lady, and ladies don't work."

"I ain't no lady."

Becket gave an indulgent laugh. "If Lady Rose could hear you now! You're slipping back into your old speech."

"I mean it. Why can't I work?"

"Because," said Becket severely, "you'll be too busy being a wife and mother."

"Mother," echoed Daisy faintly.

"As soon as I get round to it, I'm going to fix up one of the spare bedrooms as a nursery."

A scream rose up inside Daisy, but she fought it down and said, "I'll need to go to bed. I'm still not feeling well."

"You go ahead. I'll clean up here."

I'm trapped, thought Daisy miserably as she crawled into bed, and I don't know what to do about it.

The exodus to Stacey Court took place the following week. Masters and servants and mountains of luggage made their stately procession out of London. It was one of those grey weeping British days with a fine drizzle falling from the sky.

Daisy would have liked to travel with Rose, but in her new diminished status, she and Becket had to travel with the upper servants.

Stacey Court was a Tudor building, its rose-red walls covered in creepers and with many mullioned windows. In Tudor times, the more windows, the higher the status of the owner.

It was dark and damp inside. The earl ordered fires to be lit in all the rooms although it was warm outside. He had a fear of rheumatism and blamed his secretary for not having had the foresight to air and warm the place before they arrived, unaware that Matthew had suggested it to Lady Polly and had been told that as it was summer, such preparations were not necessary.

Daisy and Becket were given a room on a half landing below the servants' quarters in the attics.

Another dark place, thought Daisy miserably as she unpacked. In the servants' hall that evening, she and Becket received a warm welcome from the other servants. Brum smiled and suggested that after dinner, perhaps Mr. and Mrs. Becket could entertain them as they had done before, Becket playing his concertina and Daisy singing music hall songs.

Daisy was about to agree but Becket said severely, "I do not like my wife performing in public."

"It's not public," protested Daisy. "We're with friends."

Becket shook his head and said firmly, "I'm sorry. It would not be suitable."

A vision of the chirpy, cheery Bernie rose in Daisy's mind and again she felt that suffocating feeling of being trapped.

Upstairs, at the dinner table, the earl said to his daughter, "Captain Cathcart will be arriving tomorrow. He wanted to come and I could hardly refuse."

Rose felt a jolt of fear. She knew Harry was probably going to propose marriage. This is what she had wanted. Why did she not want it now?

After dinner, she sent a footman with a note asking Daisy to join her.

When Daisy entered, Rose hugged her. "I miss you."

"Me, too."

"Captain Cathcart is calling tomorrow. I think he means to ask for my hand in marriage."

"There you are," said Daisy bracingly. "We'll both be married ladies."

"I don't think I want to get married," said Rose.

"Go on with you! The pair of you are so well suited."

"I'm sick of danger, Daisy. I'm sick of being frightened. If I marry Harry, I will be drawn into his life."

"You don't need to be," said Daisy.

"Then what if, after we get married, another Dolores comes along?"

"Or another Roger," Daisy pointed out.

"Oh, that was such a mistake. But I would never have known how weak he was if that terrible woman hadn't threatened to kill us."

"How do you mean, 'weak'?"

"He wanted to leave me with her to get shot as long as he could escape."

"Well, they're not all like the captain."

"True. Or your Becket."

Daisy leaned forward and poked the fire. A wind had risen and was howling in the chimney. "I'm in trouble, Rose, and I don't know what to do."

"Why? What is the matter?"

"I don't love him any more. I'll have to spend the rest of my days in the gloomy flat in Bloomsbury, having one baby after another, and that's if I *can* have babies. Who knows? It might be one miscarriage after another. I'll be an old woman before my time."

"Daisy, dear Daisy. You've had a very bad shock. After a bit of rest and quiet, you'll feel differently."

"No, I won't. I know I won't. I'm frightened of beginning to hate him. Divorce isn't for the likes of us. Unless he dies, I'm stuck with him."

"You can hardly kill him," said Rose.

"Can't I?" howled Daisy. "Just you wait and see. And there's worse."

"Than wanting to kill your husband?"

"I've met someone else. It's Bernie King who works for the captain."

"His new servant?"

"No, his new detective. Oh, Rose, he's light and easy and Cockney like myself. He's fun. He makes me laugh."

"Daisy, listen to me. It is all a reaction to what you have gone through."

"Do you think you could ask the captain to suggest to Becket that I go out to work? I'm sure that would make all the difference."

"Yes, of course I shall. Now, your husband will be wondering where you are."

Rose waited anxiously the next day for Harry's arrival. What should she say to him? If she refused his proposal now that he appeared to have her parents' permission, he would never ask her again and she would probably never see him again.

The weather had cleared up and pale sunlight streamed in through all the windows.

She paced up and down the gardens, hoping to tire herself out so that she would feel calmer.

"Look at her!" said Lady Polly as she and her husband watched from the window as Rose paced up and down. "She's got permission to marry the wretched man and she looks miserable. If we mention India to her again, she'll accept him just to get out of it."

"I'm weary of the whole business," said the earl. "Rose has been such a disappointment. She'll have her own money by the time she's twenty-one. Perhaps we should accept the fact that she's going to be an old maid."

"But what a waste of all that beauty," sighed Lady Polly.

"I hear that motor of his," said the earl.

Rose had obviously heard the sound as well because she looked alarmed and then fled into the house.

"Better go and welcome him," said the earl.

• • •

Harry took tea with the earl and countess, wondering all the time where Rose had got to. The murders were not referred to. Now that the case was over, the earl and countess considered talk of murder in their drawing room very bad form.

Putting his teacup down in the saucer with an impatient little click and wondering if Lady Polly meant to talk all day about the weather, Harry said, "May I see Lady Rose? You know why I have come."

They both rose to their feet. "We'll send her to you," said the earl.

Harry waited, pacing up and down much as Rose had done in the garden.

Rose came quietly into the room. She was wearing a white lace gown with a high, boned lace collar. Her brown hair was piled up on top of her head and her blue eyes looked larger than ever.

This is it, thought Rose. What am I to do? What am I to say?

Harry took one of her hands in his. "My darling Rose," he said. "Would you—

Brum gave a loud cough. "What is it?" demanded Harry.

"There is a police inspector has called and insists on seeing you urgently."

"Tell him to wait."

"I fear he has come to arrest you, sir."

"What nonsense. Wait here, Rose. I won't be long."

Harry followed the butler down the stairs.

"I have put the person in the study," said Brum in lugubrious tones.

Harry opened the study door and walked in. A police inspector rose to meet him, flanked by two police officers.

"Captain Cathcart," he said, "we must ask you to accompany us to the police station for questioning."

"What is this about?"

"At the police station, sir. Come along. We don't want to put the cuffs on you."

Harry was taken to the market town of Hidwell and ushered into an interview room.

Daisy was sitting in the housekeeper, Mrs. Henry's, parlour, having a cup of tea. She was privately hoping Rose would be successful in persuading Harry to talk to Becket and get permission to work. The news of Harry's departure had not yet filtered below stairs.

"Must have been awful losing your baby," said Mrs. Henry, a woman as fat and comfortable as a well-worn sofa.

"You know, I don't want babies," said Daisy. "Is that unnatural?"

"Not after all you've been through."

"It's all right for the men," complained Daisy. "If they don't want babies, they can wear a condom."

The condom had been around since the time of the Egyptian pharaohs. Some say it was named after Dr. Condom, who supplied Charles II with animal-tissue sheaths.

"There is a country way for women," said Mrs. Henry.

"What's that?"

"You get a piece of green elm and stick it up your whatsit. The wood expands and blocks everything."

"I wouldn't know green elm. Can you get me some?"

"If you're sure, m'dear. Seems bit hard on your man."

"I would only use it for a little."

"I'll see what I can do."

I am Inspector Robinson," said the inspector, facing Harry across a table scarred with cigarette burns and tea stains. "You visited Miss Thomson, the woman accused of the murders, last evening, did you not?"

"Yes, I did."

"Why?"

"I was curious about her state of mind. I had begun to consider writing a book on the criminal mind."

"And she was well when you saw her?"

"Spitting venom, but otherwise fairly well. What is this about?"

"Half an hour after you left her bedside, she was found stabbed to death."

"Good heavens, man, that had nothing to do with me!"

"We checked with the prison hospital and you, sir, were the last to see her."

The questioning went on and on and then finally Harry was told they would be holding him overnight. He was formally charged with the murder of Thomson. Before he was led off to the cells he called his lawyer, who promised to be there first thing in the morning.

One of the policemen told his wife that evening of the arrest and the gossip swirled out of the town and reached Stacey Court.

The earl and countess were alarmed. Rose was strictly forbidden to visit Harry.

"We must get her away from here," said the earl, "or Rose will decide to elope with a jailbird."

"She can't elope with him if he's locked up."

"Superintendent Kerridge is a friend of Cathcart's and will probably get him released. We must get her away. Let's take her up to Tarrach as fast as possible." Tarrach was the earl's hunting lodge in Perthshire. "I'll get Matthew to make all the arrangements."

Daisy tried not to feel too selfishly upset when Rose told her that there had been no time to speak to Harry about Becket. "And you are going away tomorrow," mourned Daisy.

She looked hopefully at Rose. "We could run away again."

"I'm afraid I can't face running away any more. The stay in Scotland will help me to make up my mind about Harry."

Becket called early in the morning at the police station with a change of clothes for Harry.

"This is ridiculous," raged Harry. "I am being moved to London. My lawyer couldn't get hold of Kerridge. I thought Lady Rose might have tried to see me."

"Lady Rose was refused permission and the family are leaving for Scotland today."

Harry fretted all the way to London and when he found himself locked up in a police cell in Pentonville Prison, he felt he was moving through a nightmare.

In the evening, a guard told him he was wanted in the governor's office. Harry followed him along the bleak corridors and down the iron staircase to the governor's office.

When he walked in, Kerridge was waiting. "My dear fellow," said Kerridge, "this has all been a terrible mistake. We've caught the culprit, a hospital porter. It turns out he has a history of insanity. A nurse who was off duty when you were arrested saw him go into Thomson's room. We found the knife that stabbed her on the floor and it had his fingerprints on it."

"Wasn't there a policeman on guard outside her door?" asked Harry.

"I'm afraid he had fallen asleep. We are so sorry."

"You don't begin to know what you have done," said Harry. "Now get me out of here!"

Becket was waiting for him in the car outside. "Home, sir?"

"No, back to Stacey Court as soon as possible."

"I am afraid it is too late. The family left for Scotland this morning."

Harry felt bitter. He knew that Rose could be courageous and resourceful. She could have escaped from the house somehow and she could have come to see him.

It was finished. She did not care for him.

It was a mellow summer in Perthshire. Rose went with her parents to various parties and exercised by walking on the moors. She knew she should feel relieved, and yet she felt dull and empty. She had read about the false arrest of Harry in the newspapers. She had also read about the successful opening of Miss Friendly's salon, which had been delayed for a few weeks because a supply of brocade had not arrived in time, and experienced a pang of guilt that she had forgotten all about the opening.

She tried to tell herself that she was better off—and safer—without him, but she felt like a coward. She knew she should have escaped from Stacey Court and gone to see him.

One evening, she attended a grand ball given at the home of the Duke of Perthshire. As she whirled about the ballroom floor, Rose began to wish irrationally that Harry would walk in. She had wanted a peaceful social life and now she had it. Then she saw a man with his back to the ballroom standing at the entrance. He was tall and dark. Then he turned round and her heart sank. She had thought it was Harry.

Rose began to feel as if she had lost something very valuable.

This is a handsome sideboard, is it not?" demanded Becket.

"Yes," said Daisy, looking up from the romance she was reading.

Becket ran a finger across the surface and held it up accusingly. "See? Dust! You've got nothing else to do all day. The least you could do is to keep the place clean."

"Oh, clean it yourself. I'm bored being stuck here."

Becket bent over her. "You are my wife and you will do what I say. When I return this evening, I want this place to be spotless. Do you hear me?"

"Stop shouting. They can probably hear you over at Tower Bridge."

Becket crammed on his bowler hat and stormed out.

Daisy sighed. She looked thoughtfully at the phone.

On impulse, she picked it up and asked to be connected to Harry's office. She asked the secretary if she could speak to Mr. King.

"Who is calling?"

"Mrs. Aymes."

"One moment."

Bernie's voice came on the line. "It's me, Daisy," she whispered. "Care to meet me in Lyons for a cup of tea?"

"Hour's time, Mrs. Aymes," said Bernie.

"Who was that?" asked Harry, who had just walked into the office.

"A Mrs. Aymes," said Bernie. "Friend of my mother's. I'm taking her for a cup of tea at the Lyon's in Victoria in an hour's time, if that's all right with you, sir."

"Yes, I can't see why not."

Daisy was just about to leave when there was a knock at the door. When she opened it, it was to find Becket there accompanied by a squat woman. Becket was carrying a large bunch of red roses.

"What's this?" asked Daisy.

"This is Mrs. Blodge, who will do the cleaning."

"I'll start in the kitchen," said Mrs. Blodge cheerfully. "I allus starts in the kitchen."

Becket handed Daisy the bouquet. "I'll show you the kitchen. Wait there, Daisy. I see you're dressed to go out. But I need to talk to you."

Daisy waited nervously. She put the roses down on a side table. Becket came back.

"I've given Mrs. Blodge a spare set of keys," he said. "She can let herself out." He took Daisy's hands in his. "When I was walking away from here, I heard my own voice and the things I said to you, and I was that ashamed of myself. We used to have fun, Daisy, and it's a long time since I've heard you laugh. I phoned the captain and I've got the day off. We're going out for a slap-up lunch, champagne—the lot. Can you forgive me?"

He hung his head.

Daisy felt a great wave of relief sweeping through her. She leaned forward and kissed Becket on the cheek and said, "Come on, love. We'll let bygones be bygones."

Harry was walking past the Lyon's tea shop in Victoria an hour later and glanced in at the window. Bernie was sitting there alone, looking at his watch.

Harry walked into the tea shop. "She didn't arrive?"

"No," said Bernie gloomily. "I'd better get back to the office."

Once back at his desk, Harry sat with his head in his hands. In that moment, he hated Rose for the way she kept haunting him, the way he could not get her out of his head.

Bernie knocked and came in. "There's a lady to see you, captain."

"I'm busy . . . ," Harry was beginning to say when Bernie stood aside and Rose walked in.

"Why have you come?" demanded Harry harshly. "I thought you had run away to Scotland to avoid me."

"I did," said Rose quietly, "and now I have run back again. My parents will be furious. I must send them a telegram."

"Why have you come?" demanded Harry again.

Rose was dressed in a tailored blue velvet walking dress and on her shiny brown curls was a jaunty little hat tilted to one side.

She regarded him steadily and then said in a voice that shook slightly, "I have come to ask you to marry me."

He walked quickly round the desk and took her hands in his. "Do you know what you are saying? Why do you want to marry me? Are they threatening to send you to India again?"

"No," said Rose. "I-I l-love you."

He swept her into his arms and kissed her, and all the passion that he had suspected before was in Rose surged up to meet his own.

Have another glass of champagne," Becket was saying.

"I'm tiddly already," said Daisy. "Oh, well. Why not?"

"You know, Daisy. I've tried and tried. But I don't think I'm ever going to be a gentleman."

"Amen to that!" said Daisy. "Bottoms up!"

Keep reading FOR AN EXCERPT FROM
THE NEXT AGATHA RAISIN MYSTERY

Love, Lies and Liquor

COMING SEPTEMBER 2007 FROM
ST. MARTIN'S PAPERBACKS

ONE

James Lacey, Agatha Raisin's ex-husband with whom she was still in love, had come back into her life. He had moved into his old cottage next door to Agatha's.

But although he seemed interested in Agatha's work at her detective agency, not a glint of love lightened his blue eyes. Agatha dressed more carefully than she had done in ages and spent a fortune at the beautician's, but to no avail. This was the way, she thought sadly, that things had been before. She felt as if some cruel hand had wound the clock of time backwards.

Just when Agatha was about to give up, James called on her and said friends of his had moved into Ancombe and had invited them both to dinner. His host, he said, was a Mr. David Hewitt who was retired from the Ministry of Defence. His wife was called Jill.

Delighted to be invited as a couple, Agatha set out with James from their cottages in the village of Carsely in the English Cotswolds to drive the short distance to Ancombe.

The lilac blossom was out in its full glory. Wisteria and clematis trailed down the walls of honey-coloured cottages, and hawthorn, the fairy tree, sent out a heady sweet smell in the evening air.

Agatha experienced a qualm of nervousness as she drove them towards Ancombe. She had made a few visits to James in his cottage, but they were always brief. James was always occupied with something and seemed relieved when she left. Agatha planned to make the most of this outing. She was dressed in a biscuit-coloured suit with a lemon-coloured blouse and high-heeled sandals. Her brown hair gleamed and shone.

James was wearing a tweed sports jacket and flannels. "Am I overdressed?" asked Agatha.

One blue eye swivelled in her direction. "No, you look fine."

The Hewitts lived in a bungalow called Merrydown. As Agatha drove up the short gravelled drive, she could smell something cooking on charcoal. "It's not a barbecue?" she asked.

"I believe it is. Here we are."

"James, if you had told me it was a barbecue, I would have dressed more suitably."

"Don't nag," said James mildly, getting out of the car.

Agatha detested barbecues. Barbecues were for Americans, Australians and Polynesians, or any of those other people with a good climate. The English, from her experience, delighted in undercooked meat served off paper plates in an insect-ridden garden.

James rang the doorbell. The door was opened by a small woman with pinched little features and pale grey eyes. Her grey hair was dressed in girlish curls. She was wearing a print frock and low-heeled sandals.

"James, darling!" She stretched up and enfolded him in an embrace. "And who is this?"

"Don't you remember, I was told to bring my ex-wife along. This is Agatha Raisin. Agatha, Jill."

Jill linked her arm in James's, ignoring Agatha. "Come along. We're all in the garden." Agatha trailed after them. She wanted to go home.

Various people were standing around the garden drinking some sort of fruit cup. Agatha, who felt in need of a strong gin and tonic, wanted more than ever to flee.

She was introduced to her host, who was cooking dead things on the barbecue. He was wearing a joke apron with a picture of a woman's body in a corset and fishnet stockings. James was taken round and introduced to the other guests, while Agatha stood on a flagged patio teetering on her high heels.

Agatha sighed and sank down into a garden chair. She opened her handbag and took out her cigarettes and lighter and lit a cigarette.

"Do you mind awfully?" Her host stood in front of her, brandishing a knife.

"What?"

"This is a smoke-free zone."

Agatha leaned round him and stared at the barbecue. Black smoke was beginning to pour out from something on the top. "Then you'd better get a fire extinguisher," said Agatha. "Your food is burning."

He let out a squawk of alarm and rushed back to the

barbecue. Agatha blew a perfect smoke ring. She felt her nervousness evaporating. She did not care what James thought. Jill was a dreadful hostess, and worse than that, she seemed to have a thing about James. So Agatha sat placidly, smoking and dreaming of the moment when the evening would be over.

There was one sign of relief. A table was carried out into the garden and chairs set about it. She had dreaded having to stand on the grass in her spindly heels, eating off a paper plate.

Jill had reluctantly let go of James's arm and gone into the house. She reappeared with two of the women guests carrying wine bottles and glasses. "Everyone to the table," shouted David.

Agatha crushed out her cigarette on the patio stones and put the stub in her handbag. By the time she had heaved herself out of her chair, it was to find that James was seated next to Jill and another woman, and she was left to sit next to a florid-faced man who gave her a goggling stare and then turned to chat to the woman on his other side.

David put a plate of blackened charred things in front of Agatha. She helped herself to a glass of wine. The conversation became general, everyone talking about people Agatha did not know. Then she caught the name Andrew Lloyd Webber. "I do like his musicals," she said, glad to be able to talk about something. There was a little startled silence and then Jill said in a patronizing voice, "But his music is so derivative."

"All music is derivative," said Agatha.

"Dear me," tittered one of the female guests. "You'll be saying you like Barry Manilow next."

"Why not?" asked Agatha truculently. "He's a great

performer. Got some good tunes, too." There was a startled silence and then everyone began to talk at once.

I will never understand the Gloucestershire middle classes, thought Agatha. Oh, well, might as well eat. She sliced a piece of what appeared to be chicken. Blood oozed out onto her plate.

James was laughing at something Jill was saying. He had not once looked in her direction. He had abandoned her as soon as they entered the house.

Suddenly a thought hit Agatha, a flash of the blindingly obvious. I do not need to stay here. These people are rude and James is a disgrace. She rose and went into the house. "Second door on your left," Jill shouted after her, assuming Agatha wanted to go to the toilet.

Agatha went straight through the house and outside. She got into her car and drove off. Let James find his own way home.

When she reached her cottage, she let herself in, went through to the kitchen and kicked off her sandals. Her cats circled her legs in welcome. "I've had a God-awful time," she told them. "James has finally been and gone and done it. I've grown up at last. I don't care if I never see him again."

What an odd woman!" Jill was exclaiming. "To go off like that without a word."

"Well, you did rather cut her dead," said James uneasily. "I mean, she was left on her own, not knowing anyone."

"But one doesn't introduce people at parties any more."

"You introduced me."

"Oh, James, sweetie. Don't go on. Such weird behaviour." But the evening for James was ruined. He now saw these people through Agatha Raisin's small bearlike eyes.

"I'd better go and see if she's all right," he said, getting to his feet.

"I'll drive you," said Jill.

"No, please don't. It would be rude of you to leave your guests. I'll phone for a taxi."

James rang Agatha's doorbell, but she did not answer. He tried phoning but got no reply. He left a message for her to call back, but she did not.

He shrugged. Agatha would come around. She always did.

But to his amazement the days grew into weeks and Agatha continued to be chilly towards him. She turned down invitations to dinner, saying she was "too busy." He had met Patrick Mulligan one day in the village stores. Patrick worked for Agatha and he told James they were going through a quiet period.

When Sir Charles Fraith came to stay with Agatha, James began to be really worried. Charles, he knew, had once had an affair with Agatha. He dropped in and out of her life, occasionally helping her with cases. For the first time, James realized with amazement, he felt jealous. He had always taken it for granted that Agatha would remain, as far as he was concerned, her usual doting self. Something would have to be done.

So how's your ex?" asked Charles one Saturday as he and Agatha sat in her garden.

"I told you. I neither know nor care. I told you about that terrible barbecue."

"They sound like shiters but we all know weird people."

"He abandoned me! And when they all started sniggering about Andrew Lloyd Webber, he did nothing to defend me."

"Oh, well. It's nice to see you off the hook. If you *are* off the hook."

But Agatha was addicted to obsessions. Without one going on in her head, she was left with herself, a state of affairs she did not enjoy.

"So no murders these days?" asked Charles.

"Not a one. Nothing but lost teenagers and cats and dogs. I feel guilty. I persuaded young Harry Beam, Mrs. Freedman's nephew, to stay with me another year before going to university. He's finding things very dull."

"Is everyone else still with you?"

"Yes, Mrs. Freedman is still secretary. Then there's Harry, Phil Marshall and Patrick Mulligan as detectives."

"Why don't you take some time off? Go away somewhere. Get away from brooding about him next door."

"I am not brooding about him next door!"

Charles was so self-contained and neat in his impeccably tailored clothes and well-cut fair hair that Agatha sometimes felt like striking him. Nothing seemed to ruffle Charles's calm surface. She often wondered what he really thought of her.

"Anyway," Agatha went on, "I'm taking time off from the office today. Mrs. Freedman will phone me if anything dramatic happens. What's up with Andrew Lloyd Webber anyway?"

"Don't ask me. I never could understand the middle classes."

Fuelled by jealousy, James did not pause to think whether he really wanted the often-infuriating Agatha back in his life. He watched and waited until Charles left and then watched some more until he saw Agatha leaving her cottage on foot. He shot out of his own door to waylay her.

"Hullo, James," said Agatha, her small eyes like two pebbles. "I'm just going down to the village stores."

"I'll walk with you. I have a proposition to make."

"This is so sudden," said Agatha cynically.

"Stop walking so quickly. I feel we got off to a bad start. It really was quite a dreadful barbecue. So I have a suggestion to make. If you're not too busy at the office, we could take a holiday together."

Agatha's heart began to thump and she stopped dead under the shade of a lilac tree.

"I thought I would surprise you and take you off somewhere special that was once very dear to me. You see, I may have told you I've given up writing military history. I now write travel books."

"Where did you think of?" asked Agatha, visions of Pacific islands and Italian villages racing through her brain.

"Ah, it is going to be a surprise."

Agatha hesitated. But then she knew if she refused, she would never forgive herself. "All right. What clothes should I take?"

"Whatever you usually take on holiday."

"And when would we leave?"

"As soon as possible. Say, the end of next week?"

"Fine. Where are you going?"

"Back home to make some phone calls."

Inside her cottage, Agatha looked at the phone and then decided she must simply communicate such marvellous news to her friend Mrs. Bloxby, the vicar's wife. She let her cats out into the garden and then hurried off to the vicarage.

With her grey hair and gentle face, Mrs. Bloxby always acted like a sort of balm on the turmoil of Agatha's feelings.

"Come in, Mrs. Raisin," she said. "You are all flushed."

Both Agatha and Mrs. Bloxby were members of the Carsely Ladies' Society and it was an old-fashioned tradition among the members that only second names should be used.

"We'll sit in the garden," said Mrs. Bloxby, leading the way. "Such a glorious day. Coffee?"

"No, don't bother." Agatha sat down in a garden chair and Mrs. Bloxby took the seat opposite her. Please let it not be anything to do with James, prayed Mrs. Bloxby. I do so hope she's got over that.

"It's James!" exclaimed Agatha, and Mrs. Bloxby's heart sank.

"I thought you were never going to have anything to do with him again."

"Oh, it was because of that terrible party that I told you about. Well, just listen to this. He is arranging to take me on holiday."

"Where?"

"It's to be a surprise."

"Is that such a good idea? It might be somewhere you'll hate."

"He's a travel writer now and travel writers don't write about dreary places. I must lose weight if I'm going to look good on the beach."

"But how do you know you are going to the beach?"

Agatha began to feel cross. "Look, he obviously wants to make it a romantic holiday. You're a bit depressing about all this."

Mrs. Bloxby sighed. "Of course I hope you will have a wonderful time. It's just . . ."

"What?" snapped Agatha.

"It's just that James has always behaved like a confirmed bachelor and he can be quite self-centred. This holiday will be what he wants, not what he would think you would like."

Agatha rose angrily to her feet. "Well, sage of the ages, I'm off to do some shopping."

"Don't be angry with me," pleaded Mrs. Bloxby. "I most desperately don't want to see you getting hurt again." But the slamming of the garden door was her only reply.